ng
as
d.

w they went as nurses to   ns,
wh   their father was the senior doctor,
Aile   thought all her troubles were over,
but   ey were only just beginning! True, she
met Doctor John Lindsay, and he was
attr ted to her, but the course of true love
wou l not run smooth for them. Angela
soor found trouble, and it seemed that
noth ing short of a miracle could save her.

WAYWARD NURSE

Wayward Nurse

by

Helen Berry

Dales Large Print Books
Long Preston, North Yorkshire,
BD23 4ND, England.

British Library Cataloguing in Publication Data.

Berry, Helen
    Wayward nurse.

    A catalogue record of this book is
    available from the British Library

    ISBN   1-84262-308-7 pbk

First published in Great Britain in 1969
by John Gresham & Company

Copyright © Helen Berry 1969

Cover illustration © Heslop by arrangement with Allied Artists

The moral right of the author has been asserted

Published in Large Print 2004 by arrangement with
Robert Hale Ltd.

Dales Large Print is an imprint of Library Magna Books Ltd.

Printed and bound in Great Britain by
T.J. (International) Ltd., Cornwall, PL28 8RW

CHAPTER ONE

The little red sports car sped madly along the clearway in the sunshine, heading towards the Sussex coast, and Aileen Waring narrowed her blue eyes and glanced a little nervously at her twin sister Angela as the girl tried to get the last ounce of speed out of the powerful engine.

'Angela, for Heaven's sake slow down,' Aileen protested. 'You know there's a seventy-mile-per-hour limit on all roads. I saw a police car back there in a side road. You'll be getting another summons for speeding if you're not careful.'

'Don't be such an old woman, Aileen,' her sister retorted, blue eyes glinting recklessly as she glanced in the rear-view mirror and saw that the road behind was devoid of traffic. 'You said you were impatient to see Father again, didn't you? Well, I'm doing my best to get to Fairlawns as quickly as I can.'

'I want to get there in one piece,' Aileen retorted, staring ahead. 'You know what Father has said about your speeding. He really will take the car away from you unless you conform. You're just like a tearaway college girl instead of being a fully qualified nurse.'

'You sound just like Father,' Angela said firmly, glancing at Aileen. 'I sometimes wish I didn't have a twin sister. It's no joke having a female father-figure at my back all the time.'

'You've been pretty glad of me since we took up nursing. I have been useful in getting you out of your scrapes.'

'Serves you right for being staid!' There was a musical tone in Angela's voice. 'I don't know where you get that old-fashioned manner from. You sound just like Mother did before she died.'

'It's a good job one of us have some sense,' Aileen retorted. 'You're twenty-four now, Angela, not eighteen. I hope you're going to behave yourself at Fairlawns. Father has done his best for us, and it isn't every nurse who can get into a convalescent home to work.'

'Unless they have fathers like ours,' Angela said, smiling. 'I wonder what it will be like working in a place where the senior doctor is our father?'

'It will be nerve racking for me,' Aileen said knowingly. 'You'll have to be on your very best behaviour all the time. Father will stand none of your nonsense, and a convalescent home isn't the same as a general hospital in London. You will have to curb your waywardness, Angela, for all our sakes.'

'Nonsense! I'm not wayward! I might be high spirited, but you can't call that a disadvantage.'

'It's been called a lot worse than that outside of your hearing,' Aileen admitted. 'And I'm not going to tell you again that I won't stand for your impersonations any longer. You've given me my last lot of trouble with that particular trick.'

'Don't be so haughty!' Angela jeered mockingly. 'You must admit that we had some good laughs over it. Do you remember when Sister Pearce mistook me for you and told me Alan Hunter was waiting to see you in the waiting room?'

'I shall never forget it, and I don't suppose poor Alan will,' Aileen said. 'Passing yourself off as me isn't the funniest thing in the world.'

'Alan didn't think so when he learned the truth. And you should have seen his face while he was under the impression I was you. He thought you had gone mad and discarded all your maidenly inhibitions overnight. Are you writing to Alan?'

'No.' Aileen shook her head. 'We were just good friends. I'm not like you, Angela, always falling in and out of love.'

'I wonder what the male staff at Fairlawns will be like!' Angela mused.

'There's only one doctor,' Aileen retorted. 'Don't you remember him when he came down to visit Father and to look the place over?'

'That tall, dark-eyed hunk of man with the wavy black hair?' Angela nodded enthusiastically. 'I'm just dying to meet him again. But I expect all the other nurses have got a head start on us.'

'On you,' Aileen corrected. 'You can leave me out of your calculations.'

'Honestly, Aileen, I don't know what you see in life!' Angela sighed impatiently. 'Why don't you relax more? Look at the way you went through nursing training! I couldn't get your head out of those stuffy books. So what did it get you to be the top student nurse in the class? I passed, didn't I, and without half the studying you did? I'm here with you now, aren't I? We've got the same chances for promotion, haven't we?'

'I don't think so,' Aileen said slowly. 'You're going to come a bad cropper one of these days, Angela. You've been in more scrapes than the rest of the student class put together. But now we're going to Fairlawns you'll have to watch your step. Father is a real professional and he won't allow you any laxity.'

'Father and I have never seen eye to eye,' Angela said. 'You were always his favourite, Aileen.'

'That's not being fair to Father!' Aileen said quickly. 'If he seemed closer to me it was because you were never around. You couldn't spare the time from your having fun to realize that he was alive.'

'I'm not that bad! Really, Aileen! To hear you talk one would think I had been queen of the juvenile delinquents.'

'All right,' Aileen said, heaving a sigh. 'But I'm just trying to impress upon you that we're going to be under Father's eye all the time. He doesn't know the half of your escapades, and I hope he'll never learn. But you're going to have to quieten down a lot if you're to pass his critical eye. He's been looking forward for years to having us on his staff. Now the great day has come and I don't want anything to spoil his pleasure.'

'I don't want to hurt him,' Angela said slowly. 'But I'm telling you, Aileen, that I don't like the idea of being buried out in the wilds of the Sussex downs. I was quite happy at St Luke's in London. Father ought to realize that we have our own lives to lead. We took up nursing just to please him!'

'Is that the only reason you took to nursing?' Aileen demanded, and her pale blue eyes were sparkling with emotion.

'All right, keep your blouse on,' Angela said firmly. 'I know Mother was a nursing Sister, and that she and Father had a hospital romance. So I became a nurse. But I don't have to be crazy about the profession. You're a zealot as far as that is concerned, and good luck to you. I expect you'll finish up as Matron of a place like Fairlawns before you're finished. But that life doesn't appeal to me. I'm a qualified nurse now, and that should please Father. But I don't plan on spending the rest of my sweet life buried out here nursing rich old patients who would be better dead anyway. I think I've done my childish duty by training as a nurse. Father should now be satisfied that I was so dutiful, and let me off the hook.'

Aileen was silent. She had known for a long time that Angela was not the perfect type for a nurse. It was strange, seeing that they were twin sisters, just how different they were in temperament and outlook. Physically it was impossible to tell one from the other. They were the same height and build, with the same beautiful features and blue eyes. Only their hair styles were different; a concession to others that they might be identified. But even that arrangement had at times fallen victim to Angela's waywardness, and confusion had reigned in their circle until Aileen straightened out her sister's deliberate trickery. It had not been funny at school to be mistaken for one's twin sister. It was even worse when, as young women, one of them deliberately impersonated the other.

But all of that had to be in the past, Aileen thought as she watched the road ahead. She herself had been looking forward to working at Fairlawns with her father, and she thought it a great pity that Angela was not similarly affected by their father's prominent position and their own places in his scheme of things.

'We're nearly at the turn-off,' she said suddenly, and glanced at Angela's intent face. Her sister nodded, was already slowing the fast little car, and Aileen glanced across the rolling countryside that stretched away upon her left. She was going to enjoy this scenery. She liked Sussex. She wasn't Angela, who craved for the bright lights and

13

the bustle of the city. Here she could be content. All her life, ever since she had made up her mind to be a nurse like her mother, she had wanted to work with her father, and now the great day was upon her. She felt proud of her own achievements, and knew her father would feel similarly when she at last stood before him in her uniform to report that she was ready for duty.

She wished Angela would change a little for the better. Her sister was not a bad girl, and she had done well in her qualifying exams despite the fact that she naturally disliked studying. But there was a deeper side to Angela that could not be defined, and Aileen didn't like it. Her sister seemed at times completely dominated by some inner childishness that made her play tricks and act selfishly. They had both been in hot water solely because Angela could not control her impulses, and when two girls looked so much alike it was only natural that their superiors should liken the quieter one to her more exuberant sister.

'That's the road we want,' Aileen said suddenly, and Angela nodded, already slowing the car. They turned off the main road and plunged along a winding lane that compelled Angela to travel at little more than a crawl. Before they had covered a mile the girl was chafing at their inability to speed. Aileen kept glancing at her sister, smiling despite the gravity of her thoughts. Angela was the most impatient girl she had ever known.

'How far do we have to travel along here?' Angela demanded, glancing at Aileen, and in that instant a large black car appeared around a bend that lay just ahead and came speeding towards them.

'Look out, Angela!' Aileen shouted, for her sister's attention was not on the road.

Angela stared ahead, her slim wrists tensing as she summed up the situation and spun the steering wheel. The tyres screeched a nerve-shattering protest as she braked, and the car before them swerved a little as the driver put his toe down hard upon his brake pedal. The distance between their cars narrowed quickly, and there was not room to pass. But Angela saw that the grass verge was rather low and did not seem too bumpy.

'Hold tight,' she said through clenched teeth, and spun the wheel to send the car lurching off the road.

Aileen braced herself as the nearside wheels hit the verge and mounted it. The car before them was frighteningly near, slowing quickly, but it would not be able to stop in time. Aileen caught a glimpse of the driver's face behind the windscreen, and he was tense and worried as the narrow distance between them lessened still more. Then Angela got the offside wheels on to the verge and the danger of a collision was averted. But the car travelled along the verge, bumping badly, throwing Aileen forward and sideways. Her head struck the side of the car and she felt a stab of pain in her left temple. But she hung on grimly, trying to keep her face from the windscreen. Angela was fighting the steering wheel, trying to maintain control of the car, and they finally came to rest with the car tilting at an alarming angle, the nearside wheels on a steep bank, the bonnet only a few feet from an obdurate tree by a wide gate.

Dust filtered upwards from the wheels as Angela switched off the engine, and for a moment silence closed in about them. They were both shocked, and Aileen was dazed by the bump on the head. She lifted a hand to her left temple, dimly hearing Angela cursing the unknown driver.

'Are you all right, Aileen?' There was sharp concern in Angela's voice, and Aileen nodded slowly.

'Just caught my head, but I'm all right,'

16

she confirmed dazedly.

'Let's get out of the car and I'll take a look at you,' Angela said firmly. She glanced in her driving mirror. 'Good. That idiot has stopped and he's walking back to see if we're all right. Well, that suits me. I want to give him a piece of my mind. You always say I drive too fast, but I wasn't moving at half his speed. Did you see the way he came around that bend? He ought to be reported! The damned fool shouldn't be permitted to push a pram, let alone drive a car.'

Aileen followed her sister shakily, getting out of the car and straightening in the warm June sunshine. She found her vision blurred a little, and there was a tender spot on her left temple. A headache had assailed her, and there was something like a blacksmith's hammer pounding away behind her eyes.

'You blithering maniac!' Angela said shrilly. 'Did you ever pass a driving test?'

'Angela!' Aileen said. 'There's no damage done. Don't speak like that.'

'What do you mean by coming around that bend as you did?' her sister continued, ignoring Aileen. The driver had approached to within feet of her, and was standing there staring in wonder from one girl to the other. But Angela was fully aroused. In normal

17

circumstances she would have been aware of this handsome man's attractiveness, but her sister had been hurt and now she had the chance to show some outraged feelings. It was usually she who was shouted at for bad driving.

'Hold on a minute,' the man said. 'Is anyone hurt?'

'Not seriously, but my sister cracked her head and might have concussion,' Angela snapped. 'You're a road hog, and you ought to be locked up. Just think yourself lucky that this little incident didn't have a more serious ending. If I hadn't run off the road we would have collided head-on.'

'Just a moment,' the man said, his face red with anger, and he was making visible efforts to control himself. Aileen was staring at him, trying to place his familiar face, but the blow on her temple had affected her sight momentarily and his face seemed blurred. 'Let's take a look at your sister to see if she is all right. She looks badly shaken up to me.'

'A lot you care. You should think of that sort of thing before you get behind a wheel of a car instead of feeling sorry after you've almost killed us.'

'That's the limit.' The man raised his hands and let them fall helplessly to his sides. 'Which one of you was driving?'

'I was!' Angela rapped. 'But don't try to get out of it. You had no right to come around that bend in such a dangerous manner. Do you think you own the road or something?'

The man stepped around the irate Angela and approached Aileen, his dark eyes now filled with concern as he stared into her ashen face.

'Are you all right?' he demanded solicitously, the harsh edge gone from his tones. 'Is it merely a shaking up or did you hurt yourself?'

'I banged my head,' Aileen said slowly. Her head was acting strangely, and she felt for a sickening few moments that she was fainting away. The man must have thought the same thing for he slid an arm around her, his hand pushing under her arm. Aileen felt her legs give way, and the next moment the whole world seemed to tilt alarmingly, and blackness rushed into her mind with a roaring sound. But she did not lose consciousness. The man's voice seemed far away as he spoke quickly to Angela, and then the roaring sound faded and the blackness receded. Aileen came fully to her senses to find the man forcing her to sit down upon the grassy bank.

19

'Aileen,' Angela was saying. 'Are you all right?' There was an unusually gentle tone in her voice, but it was gone the next moment when she addressed the man. 'You'll pay for this if she's seriously hurt. Look at that bruise on her temple.'

'Will you be quiet for a moment?' the man demanded. 'Let me examine her.'

'I'll look after her. I'm a qualified nurse!' Angela snapped nastily.

'And I'm a qualified doctor!' The man retorted in similar tones.

Angela was shocked into silence, and Aileen felt gentle fingers probing her left temple. She kept her eyes closed, but was feeling stronger with each passing moment. She sighed heavily as she lifted her head. For a moment she couldn't see the man's face clearly, then her sight cleared and she forced a shaky smile.

'I'm all right now,' she said.

'You're concussed,' he retorted severely. 'You're badly shaken. Can you drive a car?'

'Yes!' Aileen thought it was a surprising question. 'Why?'

'Why?' He shook his head, his brown eyes glinting angrily. 'Why weren't you driving instead of this raving lunatic?'

'Of all the cheek!' Angela spluttered. 'You

were at fault for driving recklessly.'

'Did you ever pass a driving test?' the man demanded.

'Of course I did!' Angela was almost beside herself in anger.

'Do you know your traffic signs?' the man continued in a now dangerously calm voice.

'Most certainly!' There was a similar note in Angela's tones.

'Then can you tell me what a circular sign, painted red and with a horizontal white bar on it, means?'

'No entry!' Angela said triumphantly, after a moment's thought.

'Clever girl! Now can you tell me why you chose to ignore two such signs set at the junction where this lane meets the clearway?'

'What?' Angela was shocked.

'That's right,' the man resumed in icy tones. 'You are driving the wrong way in a one-way road.'

'But we came up here the last time we visited Fairlawns,' Angela spluttered.

'Perhaps you did. But road conditions change from day to day, or so your driving instructor should have explained to you. Those signs are plain enough. That was why I took all the road coming around that bend. The traffic is supposed to be going all one way, and that is in the direction I was taking. If you want to get to Fairlawns you have to take the next lane up on the left. That's one-way, too, so when you come out of Fairlawns don't go back down it.'

'I'm sorry,' Angela said contritely, and Aileen had to smile despite her headache.

'I'm sorry, too,' she said, getting slowly to her feet. 'I didn't notice the signs either. You're Doctor Lindsay, aren't you?'

'That's right.' The anger was gone from his voice now, and he was staring from one to the other, his expression showing mingled surprise and shock, and receding anger. 'And you two are Aileen and Angela, Doctor Waring's twin daughters.'

'That's right,' Angela said. 'What a way to meet!'

'Phew!' He grinned nervously, and his whole manner changed. 'What a calamity if we hadn't avoided one another!'

'It was only my presence of mind and expert driving that got us out of your way,' Angela ventured.

'You shouldn't have been in my way in the first place,' he retorted waspishly, and then grinned. 'Hey, don't let's rub each other up the wrong way. We've got to be friends. I've heard enough about you from your father.

He's asked me to go out of my way to be nice to you.'

'But don't strain yourself,' Angela said spitefully, her blue eyes gleaming as they took in his athletic figure and handsome face. 'I hope we haven't got off to a bad start, Doctor Lindsay.'

'No,' he said heavily, glancing at Aileen. 'How are you feeling now? You must be Aileen, I guess.'

'Father has really been talking about us,' Angela said with a rueful laugh. 'But how are you, Aileen?'

'I'll live,' Aileen replied shakily. 'You'd better turn your car around, Angela, in case a policeman shows up. You're not going to report this incident, are you, Doctor Lindsay?'

'No,' he said. 'That's if you feel all right.'

'I'm all right.' Aileen concealed her shakiness. 'But it was a very close thing.'

Angela went off to turn the car around, and Aileen stood at John Lindsay's side, her eyes upon his face. Now that she was seeing him again she was realizing that he had made quite an impression upon her that first time they had met. She had remembered him for several days after she and Angela had visited their father at Fairlawns. He in his turn was studying her, and there was a thin smile upon his tight lips.

'Your father is waiting to see you,' he said slowly. 'I have been hearing all about the pair of you.' He glanced at Angela as the girl started her engine. 'She's the terror, isn't she?'

'Not really.' Aileen smiled. 'She's a little more high spirited, that's all. She got quite good marks in her exams.'

'But you're the dedicated one.' He watched her face closely. 'How is one supposed to know which is which? You're certainly identical. But I did notice you've got longer hair than Angela. Do you always wear different hair styles?'

'Usually, except when Angela decides to impersonate me for some obscure trickery of her own. She's a practical joker, and there will be trouble at Fairlawns if she doesn't calm down.'

'I expect Sister Preston will clamp down upon her,' he said with a smile. 'She's a bit stern with the nurses. But I hope you'll be happy with us, Aileen. May I call you Aileen off duty? I expect we shall be seeing a lot of each other. We're quite a close-knit family at Fairlawns. There's a different atmosphere here. There's none of the bustle and strain

24

of the general hospital here.'

'That's a relief,' Aileen ventured, smiling. 'You may call me Aileen off duty. And what do I call you?'

'John.' His brown eyes seemed to glint as he smiled. 'I'm Doctor Lindsay on duty, and the terror of the nurses, as some of them no doubt will be quick, nay eager, to tell you.' He glanced at his watch. 'I must be on my way, unfortunately. I was in rather a hurry before we met.'

'So I noticed.' Aileen's blue eyes darkened as she recalled the frightening moment of his appearance around the bend.

'Thank the Lord it wasn't worse,' he told her. 'But you are looking shaky. You'd better tell your father all about it when you see him and let him take a look at you. I think you're suffering a little from concussion, and no doubt he'll order you to bed for the rest of the day.'

'That will be a nice way to start my duties at Fairlawns,' Aileen said unsteadily.

'Better to be safe than sorry,' he retorted, smiling thinly. He glanced at Angela, who had turned the car and parked it behind his. 'Off you go. It's the next turning on the left, and don't let Angela forget that it's also one-way.'

'We're not likely to forget after what's happened,' Aileen said slowly.

'That's the hard way to learn.' He took her arm, and Aileen felt a tremor pass through her at his touch. But he escorted her to the car and helped her into the seat. 'Pay more attention to your driving,' he said in severe tones to Angela, and the girl nodded soberly. 'See you later,' he ended, and turned and went back to his own car.

Aileen watched him through narrowed eyes, and her arm seemed to be burning where his fingers had held her. She watched him drive away, and then Angela followed. When they reached the main road he turned right and drove towards the village through which they had passed a short time before, and Angela turned left.

'He's a real dish,' Angela observed when they found the right turn-off. 'What did you think of him, Aileen?'

'I thought him very nice, and a pleasant man, under the circumstances that we met. Don't you start getting ideas, though, sister, because no doubt he's got a girl friend, or even a wife, and we don't want that kind of trouble dogging us in our new position.'

'Father said he wasn't married,' Angela

retorted brightly. 'I think John Lindsay is some kind of a woman hater, for some reason or other. But we'll find out, won't we?'

CHAPTER TWO

Aileen was silent as they completed their drive to Fairlawns. John Lindsay had made quite an impression upon her when they had first met, and this second meeting, although under unexpected circumstances, had refired her thoughts. She could still feel the pressure of his hand upon her arm, and there was a thrill playing along her spine as she leaned back and closed her eyes. Although she was feeling shaken by the near disaster and the bump she had received, she was more concerned with the impression John Lindsay had made in her mind, and she didn't like the way Angela was talking about him. She knew her sister only too well. Every man was fair game for Angela, and although there was no harm in her sister, Angela did not seem to realize the effect she had upon the opposite sex. There had always been a string of men behind

Angela, all clamouring for her attention, and the girl had enjoyed every minute of playing one against another.

But it had to stop now! Aileen was certain that Angela's behaviour at the hospital would not be tolerated here at Fairlawns. The convalescent home was smaller and quieter, with a list of private patients who were more genteel and sophisticated than the patients they had been accustomed to handling. But Aileen was more concerned about the effect Angela's usual behaviour would have upon their father. He knew his daughters only too well, but he didn't know the full extent of Angela's attitude towards life, and Aileen could see trouble looming upon the horizon before they had arrived.

Fairlawns had been a stately home in the distant past, and had fallen into a bad state of disrepair before it was bought and turned into a convalescent home. Aileen had fallen in love with it at first sight, and had been impatient to return here. But she knew Angela was not similarly affected. Her sister would rather have stayed on in London, and had insisted upon doing so until Aileen got to work on her. But at best she had only agreed to stay for a year at most to gratify her father's dream of having both daughters working with him. After that, Aileen knew, there would be trouble.

Angela turned into a driveway that was hemmed in by lofty trees that intermingled their branches high overhead. The tyres made a swishing sound in the gravel, and the silence that clung to the countryside was heavy and complete.

'Oh God!' Angela declared suddenly. 'This peacefulness is going to drive me crazy. How can we be so unalike in temperament, Aileen? You love this, don't you?'

'I do, and you'll get to like it in time, so don't start blocking your mind before you've had a chance to experience it,' Aileen retorted. 'Just think of Father.'

'That's all we've been doing ever since we were old enough to think for ourselves,' Angela declared rebelliously.

'He's all we've got left in the world,' Aileen responded quickly. 'If we don't care about each other then no one else will bother.'

'We've got our own lives to lead, I keep telling you,' Angela snapped. 'Father led his own life, didn't he?' She sighed heavily. 'Oh, what's the use? How can I fight the both of you? But you're my twin sister, and you at least should be able to see my point of view.'

'I do, but the trouble is I can see Father's,

too, and you can't. You're blind to other people's lives, Angela. You're not exactly selfish, but you're self-centred.'

The driveway opened out to a large expanse of gravelled ground flanked by vast lawns, and across the way stood the house, square and substantial, its front face filled with many glittering windows. Wide steps led to a large doorway, and a thick green creeper occupied most of the wall space between the windows. Dark tiles sloped under the bright blue sky, and the tall, twisted chimney pots serrated the high horizon.

Angela slowed the car as they approached, and Aileen gasped in pleasure. Her sister snorted and glanced at her, and for a moment, as their eyes held each other's gaze, Aileen could sense the thread of thought in Angela's mind, and see the turmoil in her sister's bright eyes.

'Try and like it, for Father's sake,' Aileen said, and Angela pursed her lips and shrugged.

There was a large notice on the left, advising drivers that only visitors to the patients could park before the house. Angela followed the driveway around to the rear of the sprawling building, and parked in a small space by a notice which read *Staff*

Car Park.

'Well, we've arrived,' Angela said slowly, switching off the engine and relaxing with a sigh. 'How's your head?'

'Aching a bit,' Aileen replied, opening the door and getting out of the car. She narrowed her blue eyes as she looked around. There was a profusion of tall trees, and large black shadows sprawled across the lawns and the gaily coloured flower beds. In the distance there was the bent figure of an oldish man at work on one of the flower beds, and another man was on a ladder cleaning the windows in the side of the house.

The back door opened as they approached and a tall, thin woman appeared. She paused in the doorway when she saw them, and smiled as they drew nearer.

'No need to ask who you are,' she said lightly. 'Doctor Waring's daughters. Do come in, and I'll get the porter to bring in your cases. Doctor Waring asked me to watch for you, and I'll take you straight along to his office. I'm Mrs Palmer, the cook.'

'How do you do?' Aileen acknowledged. 'I'm Aileen and this is Angela.'

'I don't know how we shall tell you apart,' Mrs Palmer said with a smile.

'It's only when we're together that people

have any real trouble in identifying us,' Angela murmured.

'Well, come this way and I'll take you to your father. He is expecting you.'

Angela smiled at Aileen as they followed the woman into the building, and Aileen looked around eagerly at the large, spotlessly clean kitchen. There was a young woman at work at the far end, but although she looked up at them Mrs Palmer made no introduction. They went through an inner doorway and entered the front of the house. Smooth high walls were painted white, and the tiled floors were highly polished. Before them lay the imposing front entrance, and they passed under the curving flight of stairs that led to the upper part of the building.

Aileen looked around with interest, and there was a leaping eagerness inside her at the thought of seeing her father again. But a glance at Angela's face did not reassure her. Angela was not going to like it here, and her sister had no intention of pretending that she did.

They walked along the ground-floor corridor and paused at a door bearing their father's name. Mrs Palmer smiled at them as she tapped at the door. She stepped away as a gruff voice gave an invitation to enter.

'He's in,' she said. 'I hope you'll both be very happy here.' She hurried away as Angela opened the door, and Aileen followed her sister into the office.

Robert Waring was a tall, powerfully built man of fifty-six, and it was easy to see where Aileen and Angela got their blue eyes and other physical characteristics from. He looked up at their entrance, then put down his pen and got quickly to his feet, coming around the desk with an eagerness he did not conceal.

'Aileen, Angela! You're here at last!' His long arms opened and he gathered both girls in his embrace, hugging them to his chest and kissing them.

Aileen felt deep pleasure flood through her, and she clung to him like a small child. One of his large hands lifted to her hair and ruffled it playfully. Angela struggled free of the embrace, and there was a thin smile upon her lips as she stepped back.

'Father, we're not schoolchildren home on holiday,' she said.

'You wouldn't deny your father the pleasure of showing his happiness, would you?' he demanded, smiling broadly. 'I've waited a long time for this moment, I can tell you.' He stared first at Angela, then at

Aileen, and a frown appeared between his blue eyes when he looked at Aileen. 'Hello,' he said. 'You look a bit under the weather, my girl. Is anything wrong?'

Angela explained what had happened, and Robert Waring took Aileen's arm and led her towards a chair set by a large window. Aileen sat down and permitted her father to examine the bruise on her left temple. He stared into her eyes for a moment, then nodded.

'A slight case of concussion,' he announced. 'Perhaps we had better send you to bed for the rest of the day.' His pale eyes lifted to Angela's intent face. 'Still driving as recklessly as ever?' he demanded quietly.

'That's not fair, Father!' she retorted. 'Aileen didn't see those no entry signs either.'

'But Aileen wasn't driving,' he said, shaking his head. 'But all's well that ends well, eh, Angela? That seems to be your attitude towards life.' He paused and looked from one beautiful face to the other, seeing adoration in Aileen's eyes and a shadow of rebellion in Angela's. He smiled. 'But never mind that. You're here now and we want to make the best of it. I hope you'll both settle down with us. You'll find your duties very easy after what you've been accustomed to. The staff are very good, and we're just like one big happy family. Matron is away on a week's holiday this week, and Sister Preston is in charge. I don't know how you'll make out with Sister Preston. She is a bit of the old-school type, if you know what I mean, but she's got a heart of gold beneath her harsh exterior. We'll go along and meet her presently.'

'I'm looking forward to starting,' Aileen said. 'The scenery around here is wonderful, Father.'

'I love this part of the country,' he retorted. 'I'm sure you'll both settle down without difficulty. We'll be able to spend some time together now. It will make a change after all these past years. The time seemed endless, waiting for you both to finish your studies and get some experience. But you're both here now, and I'm sure your mother would have been very proud of you had she been spared to see you today.'

Aileen felt tears prickle at the back of her eyes, but Angela moved impatiently.

'We're here now, Father,' Angela said. "What duties do we get, and where are our rooms?'

'Of course, you want to get settled in. There'll be plenty of time later for us to talk. Come along and I'll find one of the maids to show you to your rooms, and the porter will bring up your luggage. You'll both be working during the day, although later you'll take your turns at night duty with the other nurses. There are two other day nurses here, and I'm sure you'll find them both very friendly. We had two temporaries working with us, holding your positions for you, and they departed at the end of last week. You'll be commencing in the morning.'

'That will suit me,' Aileen said. 'How many patients are there, Father?'

'Forty-eight at the moment,' he replied. 'There are twenty-seven men and twenty-one women. But I'll leave Sister Preston to sort out your duties. She's an efficient Sister, and I'm sure you'll both like her.'

'We always like Sisters,' 'Angela said with a thin smile.

Robert Waring moved to the door and opened it. He was smiling warmly, and Aileen could see that he was really happy with their arrival. She felt a warmth building up inside her at the knowledge that his years of waiting were at an end, but there was a thread of worry tying knots in the back of her mind as she glanced at Angela's tense expression.

Blanche Preston was a tall, robust woman

in her middle thirties, and her narrowed brown eyes studied Aileen and Angela critically when Robert Waring introduced them.

'They're a credit to you, Doctor Waring,' she said in a strong voice. 'I'm sure we'll all get along very well indeed. You can leave them in my hands now and I'll see that they get settled in.'

'Very well, Sister Preston,' he replied, smiling fondly at them. 'I'll see you both later and we can have a talk. We'll get together this evening. If there's anything you want, then don't hesitate to ask Sister Preston or come to me.'

'Thank you, Father,' Angela said. She glanced at Aileen, and went on, 'We're both very happy to be here with you.'

'And I'm happy to have you,' he retorted, turning away.

Aileen smiled as she watched him depart. He was happy, and she knew he had been leading an almost empty life since their mother had died. She knew sadness as she followed Angela and the Sister along the corridor and up the back stairs to what had once been the servants' quarters. They were shown into small adjoining rooms that were well furnished, and Sister Preston left them, promising to send up the porter with their luggage. When the sister's heavy footsteps had receded Angela appeared in Aileen's doorway.

'Well, we're here,' Angela said heavily. 'I suppose I'd better make the most of it. But this will be like a prison to me, Aileen. I don't like it, I tell you.'

'Perhaps you'll get used to it,' Aileen replied. 'You have nothing in London to attract you. You didn't fall in love with anyone, did you? Your heart isn't being held elsewhere.'

'You know I haven't found that dream man yet,' Angela said.

'You've certainly done enough looking for him.' There was a slight tone of reproach in Aileen's voice, and Angela laughed harshly.

'A girl is only young once, sister,' she retorted. 'If I'm to be buried alive here, then I'm going to need those memories of mine to help me through. There must be something wrong with you if you do like this sort of thing. There's something missing from your mental make-up, I shouldn't wonder.'

'Well, don't start playing games to help you pass the time,' Aileen warned. 'Father has a responsible position here, and your kind of humour and joke-playing could only embarrass him. We're not at the hospital now.'

'And don't I know it!' Angela sighed heavily. 'What about Sister Preston? She looks a real sergeant-major. I didn't like that glint in her eyes as she greeted us. I think I know her kind. She's going to hold it against us that Father is the senior doctor here.'

'Nonsense. She looks a thoroughly efficient Sister to me. But she won't stand any nonsense, so you'll have to watch your step.'

'Give up hope all ye that enter here!' Angela said slowly.

Footsteps sounded in the corridor, and the next moment a young man wearing a long brown dust coat appeared in the doorway, loaded down with the cases he had taken from their car. He dropped the cases to the floor and straightened, staring from one to the other, and the look of admiration and surprise that came to his face made Angela laugh.

'Crikey!' he exclaimed, blue eyes alight with interest. 'Things are looking up. I've heard of identical twins, but you two take the biscuit. How are we to know who's who?'

'I'm Aileen and this is Angela.' Aileen smiled as she went forward to take her two cases. 'You'll soon get to know us.'

'I hope so,' he said cheekily. 'You're two very welcome additions to the staff. You'll put Joanne Gould's nose out of joint, no doubt. You'll need to watch out for her. If she takes a dislike to you she'll make you sorry you were ever born.'

'And who is Joanne Gould?' Angela demanded stiffly.

'She's one of the nurses,' came the quick reply. 'She's got her eye on Doctor Lindsay, but he won't have any of it. Have you met him yet?'

'We have,' Angela said. 'Would you take my cases into the next room, please? And what do we call you?'

'I'm Pat Carmell, the porter. Anything you want around here, then call for me. I know what's going on all the time. I've got a mate, but he's off duty at the moment. He's the night porter this week. But he's an old man and very old fashioned. I'm the boy for getting things done around here. I suppose you've met Sister Preston?'

'Yes, we've met her, and don't tell me, she's just as bad as she looks,' Angela said. 'We've met her kind before.'

'She's not a bad old sort so long as you do as you're told,' he said with a grin, his blue eyes bright with admiration. 'Any chance of a date with either of you?' He laughed jocularly. 'I don't suppose it matters which of you a fellow takes out. You're both exactly the same. I should imagine that sort of thing can present problems to the man and also to you girls.'

'We haven't noticed yet,' Angela said thinly, leading the way out of the room, and Carmell smiled impishly at Aileen and followed, carrying Angela's bags.

Aileen could hear him chatting to Angela as she unpacked and began to put away her clothes. She sighed heavily once or twice, her thoughts upon her sister. She wanted dearly for this to work out for her father's sake, but she knew Angela well enough to realise that her sister was not satisfied, and she wondered how long Angela would be able to content herself here.

As she settled in, her mind returned to the incident on the road, and Aileen felt her heartbeats quicken as she considered John Lindsay. Her arm tingled where his fingers had gripped it, and recollection of his darkly handsome face and brown eyes made her sigh deeply. She had never met a man who could really attract her! Her boyfriends had been just that, friendly. She had never entered into an emotional association with any of them, and it had begun to affect her outlook, the inner knowledge that she had been incapable of loving. But Angela had never suffered from that particular incapacity. There had always been rumours about Angela's love life in the hospital. The girl lived life to the full, and that was the main reason why Aileen felt so disturbed. She knew in her heart that Angela would not settle down in this quiet position, and someone would get hurt when the girl finally decided to make a break. Her father would be the one to suffer, and Aileen didn't like the thought of that.

She turned to look at Angela as the girl walked in through the doorway. Her sister was smiling thinly, but there was an expression in her pale eyes that warned Aileen.

'All settled in?' Angela demanded. 'I've put away my clothes. But tell me, where do we go when we're off duty? I saw a village about four miles back along the road, and the nearest town is Whitebay, isn't it? That's a long way from here. It's a one-horse place, too, from what I know about it. How long do we have to stay here, Aileen? When will Father be satisfied and cut us loose?' She smiled thinly. 'We're big girls now, and even the birds can leave their nests when they're old enough to fly. What's so different about us?'

'It's something in the mind,' Aileen responded slowly. 'I have it. It's an urge to stay with Father and to try and make his life a little happier. He's been dreadfully lonely since Mother died. But if you don't feel that, Angela, then obviously you don't know what I'm talking about, and I suppose you'll never be able to settle down here. But that is something between you and Father. Only try not to hurt him when you decide to break loose. I know you think the world of him, but you're not very tactful at the best of times.'

'I know what you're trying to say,' Angela retorted. 'I like the sentiments behind your thinking, dear, but it just does not work. I'm not happy about it, and I'm sure Father wouldn't want me to stay if it made me unhappy. But I'll give it a trial, don't you think I won't. I'll have to stay six months at least, so you needn't start worrying that I'll be up and away like a grasshopper. Come on, let's go down and see if there's any tea going. It won't take us long to get into the routine here, and no doubt I can use my talents to liven things up a bit.'

'That's exactly what I'm afraid of,' Aileen said with a laugh.

They held hands as they went down the stairs together.

CHAPTER THREE

It didn't take them long to settle in, as Angela had guessed. The very next morning they started their duties, and as in the hospital they had left, the routine was everything. Going on duty for the first time was like boarding a slowly moving train that immediately picked up speed. There was no let-up, and time seemed a secondary thing, subservient to duty. There was much for them to learn. They had to meet the patients and memorise names and case histories. They had to learn their way around and meet their colleagues. Sister Preston soon impressed upon them the nature of her efficiency and the method she used to ensure competency in her subordinates. Although she never raised her voice the Sister managed to project her true nature. Sarcasm was her chief weapon, and Angela soon felt the edge of the Sister's soft whip of a tongue.

The two nurses with whom they shared day duties proved to be of widely differing natures. Joanne Gould was a plumpish girl of medium build, with brown eyes and long unruly brown hair that refused to stay up under her small cap. It soon became a regular feature to see Joanne walking along the corridors vainly trying to tuck her hair up and loose ends showed no matter what she did. But Sally Collins was a tall, slim brunette with an attractive, heart-shaped face, and Aileen took to her from the very first moment they were introduced. The girl was a smiler, and her white teeth made her habit an attractive mannerism. Sally felt a kindred emotion for Aileen, and at the end of the first week a close relationship had sprung up between them. But Aileen could not get along with Joanne Gould. The girl was secretive, and after the first few days showed a tendency towards jealousy against the twin sisters. Angela didn't waste any time before she tackled Joanne, and Aileen was horrified to hear their raised voices one afternoon coming from the little room that served as an office and kitchen. Before she could intervene in the role of peacemaker

Sister Preston appeared in the corridor and hurried in to bring her own brand of peacemaking into effect.

Sally Collins kept her eyes lowered as she left a patient's room, but Aileen reached out a hand and caught hold of the girl's arm.

'What's the matter between Angela and Joanne?' she demanded. 'Do you have any idea, Sally?'

'They're squabbling over who will attend Doctor Lindsay when he comes around,' the girl replied.

'That's something to fight over, I must say!'

Sally threw Aileen a quick, frowning glance. 'Don't you like Doctor Lindsay?' she demanded.

'Of course I do, but I wouldn't make an enemy of a nurse just to walk around at his side,' Aileen retorted.

'I like Doctor Lindsay,' Sally said slowly, and there was a strange expression in her dark eyes. 'I wish Angela was more like you, Aileen. I think she's beginning to set her cap at the doctor, and that isn't going to give the rest of us much chance.'

'Nonsense! You're a very attractive girl, Sally!'

'Perhaps, but without the advantages of a

father who is the senior doctor here.'

'Would that sort of thing count with Doctor Lindsay?' Aileen shook her head slowly. 'I wouldn't have thought so. If it did then I wouldn't want to know him.'

'You and Angela are so different,' the girl went on. 'I like you. I think you're a very nice person, but I can't take to Angela in the same way despite the fact that the two of you can't be told apart. I've known you a week now and I still call you Angela. How can I know the difference, Aileen?'

'Look,' Aileen said, smiling. She lifted her blonde hair to expose her right ear. 'Can you see that little scar on the lobe? Angela did that to me when we were girls. She lost her temper and hit me with a teacup.'

'Well, that's nice!' Sally shook her head. 'But I can't look at your ear every time I meet you. What would Angela think if I lifted her hair one morning and looked at her ear?'

'I don't know what Angela would think,' said a voice behind them, 'but I shall certainly remember that for future reference.'

Aileen turned quickly, and her heart seemed to miss a beat when she saw John Lindsay standing within earshot. How much had he heard of their conversation?

47

She glanced at Sally, to see that the girl was blushing badly. Sally turned to go about her duties, and as Aileen followed John Lindsay called to her.

'You are Aileen, aren't you?' he demanded.

'Yes, Doctor.' She paused, catching Sally's backward glance as the girl continued on her way.

'Let me have a look at that scar on your ear.' He came to her side and lifted her hair, peering intently at the small scar on the tiny lobe. 'It's a very pretty ear,' he mused gently.

Aileen stepped back, her face turning scarlet for some unknown reason, and as she realised it she felt more confused that ever. She never blushed! Her breathing was unsteady as she watched him.

'Thank you for the compliment,' she said thickly.

'What was all the fuss about?' he demanded. 'The fuss that Sister Preston has gone to quell!' His dark eyes seemed to bore right through Aileen. 'Is it true what Nurse Collins just said?'

'About what?' Aileen was giving nothing away. 'Did you hear what was said?'

'Most of it,' he admitted with a smile. He seemed to tower over her as he stood by her side, and she was too conscious of his good looks. 'Well, if you won't tell me then I shall have to rely upon my own keen sense of hearing. Sally said Angela and Nurse Gould are fighting over which of them should accompany me on my round. Isn't that correct?'

'That's right,' Aileen admitted reluctantly.

'So that's the state of affairs!' He nodded slowly, and Aileen could detect a glint in his brown eyes. 'Well, we can't have one getting jealous of the other, so I think you'd better come with me this morning. Sister Preston seems to be busy, and I wouldn't want to drag her away from some matter of discipline. But tell me why you're not in there arguing for your chance to accompany me?'

'I'm afraid I'm not a girl like that,' Aileen retorted.

'Don't be afraid because of it,' he said gently. 'I'm glad. I don't like to be the cause of unrest among the nurses. But tell me more. Am I not your type? Is that the reason why you're not interested?'

'It isn't that at all, Doctor.' Aileen tried to control her fast-beating heart. If only he knew just how much he confused her!

'It couldn't be that you still hold me responsible for that near accident that occurred the day you arrived?'

'Certainly not! It wasn't your fault at all.

What kind of a girl do you think I am? Do you believe I would hold something like that against you?'

'Don't sound so forceful,' he replied with a laugh. 'I didn't mean it. But come along and we'll start my round. I want to talk to you when it's over. Do you know that before you arrived your father asked me to go out of my way to be nice to you and your sister?'

'Really?' Aileen tried to keep her tones unconcerned. 'I think he must have had a tactless moment.'

'He was probably thinking of Angela when he said it,' John Lindsay said with a laugh. 'And he's quite right. A man like me would have to go out of his way to be nice to a girl like Angela.' He held up a hand, backing off a step in mock alarm. 'Now don't get me wrong,' he went on quickly. 'There's nothing wrong with your twin sister! It's just that she's definitely not my type.'

'I think I know what you mean,' Aileen conceded with a smile. 'She is rather intense.'

'That's a good word for it!' He nodded slowly. 'I think she's one of the most beautiful girls I've ever seen.' He paused to note the effect of his words, and when Aileen said nothing he continued. 'Which means, of course, that you are, too. But I like a girl

50

who's quiet and responsible. I would have jumped at the chance your father's words gave me if Angela had been like that, but alas she isn't the girl I'd care to spend my spare time with. She would have my nerves ragged inside of a week. It's a great pity, because for the right man she would be a great deal of fun. Now if she had a sister, someone who looked exactly like her but had a quieter nature and seemed to like the kind of things I like, then I'd jump at the chance of taking her out and getting to know her.'

Aileen said nothing, but her heart seemed to have lost its even beat. She felt as if she had suddenly become intoxicated by some fairyland mixture of happiness and hope. Her breath seemed to catch in her throat, and she could only stare at him as he smiled down at her with those wonderful lights in his dark brown eyes.

'I know this is all a roundabout way of asking you out one evening,' he said at length, 'and I do apologise. But I'm afraid that you will say no.'

Aileen lowered her gaze to hide the sudden rush of emotion to her eyes, but he reached out a swift, gentle hand and took her chin between his fingers and thumb, tilting her head and staring deeply into her blue eyes.

'Don't hide anything from me,' he said softly. 'You've got beautiful eyes. Don't say no immediately, will you? Think about it. I'd like to take you out one evening – this evening for preference – and you can let me know when we've finished the round. Now come along before Sister Preston shows her strong face out here.'

He turned and walked away, and Aileen hurried along behind him, feeling as if she were walking on air. What had happened to her? How was it that this man could arouse so many strange emotions in her? She breathed deeply, trying to steady herself, and when he turned to glance at her she was afraid that he would see the stars shining in her eyes.

But she had no time to consider her feelings. He started his round of the patients, and Aileen followed, her mind in a daze of wonder. She could not keep her gaze from his face as he talked with the patients and examined them. But he had not forgotten Aileen's presence, and she experienced a thrill each time their glances met. When they had completed the round he pulled a face. They were standing in the corridor on the second floor. Aileen heard him sigh.

'Now we've got to see our special cases. Have you met them yet, Aileen?'

'Yes, Doctor,' she replied calmly.

'I'm not going to like hearing you call me Doctor,' he said. 'But there's nothing we can do about that while we're on duty. But I want a promise from you that when we are off duty you'll call me John.'

'Certainly, Doctor Lindsay,' she replied, and he grinned.

'Come along then and we'll see how Cora Anderson is doing. You know, I think I'll make it a rule to always have you with me on my rounds. I've got done in record time today, and you have a nice way with you in handling the patients.'

'Thank you, Doctor!' Aileen lowered her gaze again, and he shook his head slowly as she coloured slightly.

They went on to the special rooms, and Aileen felt a flicker of interest stab through her as they entered Cora Anderson's. Miss Anderson was a film actress who had seen stardom in the earlier years of her career. But she had fallen upon hard times, and in her bid to make a comeback she had been sadly disillusioned by modern standards. She had taken an overdose of sleeping tablets in an attempt to end her misery, but had been prevented from dying. Now she was in the care of Robert Waring and his staff, and coming along very nicely. She had already recovered from her desire to die. All that remained now was to give her reason to live.

'Well, Miss Anderson,' John Lindsay said as he entered the room. 'What kind of a night did you have?'

'Fine, thank you,' came the terse reply, and Aileen searched the ageing face for signs of distress. But the woman's faded blue eyes were expressionless. 'Where is Doctor Waring this morning?'

'He's off duty at the moment, but if you wish to see him, then I'll let him know.'

'It doesn't matter, Doctor. I'm as well as can be expected.'

'Are you feeling well?'

'I think I shall pass muster,' came the tense reply. The woman's eyes came to Aileen's face, held for a moment, then swept over the girl's lithe, youthful figure. Something of a nostalgic smile came to the wrinkled face. 'If you could turn back the clock perhaps thirty years I should be very much happier,' she remarked.

'This is Nurse Waring,' John Lindsay said brightly. 'She is Doctor Waring's daughter.'

'We have already met.' There was coldness in the direct glance that came Aileen's way. 'I have asked this nurse to stay away from my room.'

Doctor Lindsay glanced at Aileen in some surprise, and she shook her head.

'Not me,' she said apologetically. 'You must mean my sister Angela, Miss Anderson.'

'We have twin nurses on our staff, Miss Anderson,' Doctor Lindsay said. 'I can personally vouch for Aileen.'

The faded blue eyes studied Aileen's face. Then there came a faint nod. 'I can see now that this is not the same nurse,' Cora Anderson said. 'This one has a much gentler nature.'

'I must compliment you upon your perception,' John Lindsay said with a smile. 'Not many people can tell the girls apart, except Doctor Waring. Sometimes I even wonder if the girls themselves know which they are.'

'It's not quite as bad as that,' Aileen said with a laugh.

They went on, and in another room Aileen saw Paul Raynor, a novelist in his early forties who had suddenly lost the ability which had made his name in the realms of science fiction. A nervous breakdown had robbed him of his mental clarity, and he seemed like a drugged man as he sat in an easy chair by the window, staring out over the rolling downs that stretched away at the rear of the house. He answered Doctor Lindsay's questions in monosyllables, and did no more than let his eyelids flicker when he half glanced towards Aileen.

When they left the room Aileen touched John Lindsay's arm. 'Will he ever recover?' she demanded.

'I certainly hope so. We're doing all we can for him, but that's little enough at the moment. It's really up to Nature to repair some of the damage before we can hope to take over with any measure of success. You're really interested in all of this, aren't you?'

'Of course I am,' Aileen replied, a little surprised by his remark. 'Why do you think I took up nursing?'

'Angela came around with me yesterday,' he replied. 'I didn't need to ask her the same question. She hasn't a scrap of interest in any of this. I'm going to be a very surprised man if she stays here longer than the minimum six months.'

'That's what worries me,' Aileen admitted. 'I think it would hurt my father deeply if Angela decided to leave.'

'I know he's been looking forward to having you both here. He's been talking about it for years. I've been looking forward to meeting you again after our first meeting!'

'Really?' Aileen felt a flicker of surprise as she stared into his handsome face. He stood tall and straight before her, a rock of a man who would provide wonderful security for any girl. 'Are you sure it was not Angela?'

'I'm sure,' he said with a smile. 'I know you two girls are identical twins, but that's because most people look at you with their eyes and not their minds. I can see a great many differences in you and Angela. There are small mannerisms, and the great difference of character. I can even tell you by your walk.'

'Does that mean you've been studying us?' Aileen demanded lightly.

'Certainly. With two such girls on the staff one has to be able to tell one from the other. It must be difficult enough for the nurses, but for a man it is even worse.'

'How?' Aileen watched him closely, but his face was composed, showing nothing.

'Supposing a man fell in love with you?' There was a lift in his tones which betrayed more than a casual interest, and Aileen caught her breath. 'Would he know which was you every time?'

'I should imagine so.' Aileen smiled thinly. 'When two people fall in love I should imagine they become very close. Although Angela and I are identical, we are miles apart in personality.'

'True.' He started walking along the corridor. 'Well, I want an answer now to my invitation. Would you care to come out with me this evening?'

'I should like to,' Aileen said frankly. 'But by accepting I may be putting my life in danger.'

'How's that?' His face showed puzzlement.

'The other nurses. Don't tell me you don't know that they all adore you.'

'I've heard them talking at times,' he admitted with a grin. 'But I've always kept aloof from the staff. Getting too friendly with a nurse might have unfortunate repercussions. This is only a small place, not like a large general hospital, and it could prove awkward if personal lives intruded into duty hours.'

'But aren't you afraid that this might happen between us?' Aileen watched his face, saw him smile, and felt a warmth welling up inside her.

'I'm willing to take that risk with you,' he

said firmly. 'There are some girls who just force themselves upon a man, and you're one of them.'

'Not consciously,' she protested.

'Certainly not! You've been too much the other way. I thought I had the art of remaining aloof to a fine art, but you are a past master at it. I was beginning to think that I'd never get near you.'

'I've only been here a week,' Aileen protested with a smile.

'And that's far too long for me. Normally I'm not an impatient man, but you seem to have got under my defences. Shall I look for you at about seven?'

'I'll be ready,' she promised.

'I thought we might take in the Summer Show at Whitebay for a start, then supper afterwards at a little restaurant I know. Does that sound interesting?'

'Very.' Aileen was trying to tell herself that she was not dreaming. The week that had passed since their arrival had done more than introduce them to the routine at the home. She had been increasingly aware of John Lindsay's presence, and she had noticed that she listened intently whenever any of the nurses talked of John. She watched his tall figure as he excused himself and walked away. What was there about him that gave her so many odd emotions? She had been in the company of lots of young men, but none had been able to stir her so deeply.

Aileen walked back along the corridor, almost walking on air, she discovered to her surprise. But John Lindsay was a strikingly handsome man, and she was feeling the closeness of the unchanging atmosphere and scenery. They hadn't been out since their arrival, and Aileen told herself that if she was beginning to feel hemmed in then Angela must be fretting inwardly about their captivity. No wonder her sister was beginning to argue with the other nurses.

Sally Collins appeared from a patient's room, and there was a sad smile on her face as she waited for Aileen to come up with her. Aileen took in the girl's expression, and felt guilty as she fell into step beside her.

'I wish I were in your shoes,' Sally said tensely. 'I've never been asked by the great man himself to accompany him on his round. Sister Preston won't like it, either. You wouldn't think she was capable of human emotion, would you?'

'Is she sweet on Doctor Lindsay, then?' Aileen asked in some surprise.

'Of course she is! Tell me who isn't! You are, aren't you, Aileen?'

'I like him, naturally,' Aileen replied cautiously, and wondered how she would be able to break the news to these girls. She had to tell them that John had asked her out for the evening, and suddenly she felt overwhelmed by the knowledge. Her face took on a brightness that brought a blush to her cheeks as she considered it. She knew her blue eyes were sparkling, and her hands trembled as she took a deep breath. 'He's asked me out this evening, Sally,' she said.

The girl stopped in midstride, her face showing her surprise, and there was a tinge of disappointment, too. For a moment they stared at one another, and then the girl made an effort to control her feelings.

'Aileen, this must be a miracle,' she said. 'He's never so much as looked twice at a nurse in all the time I've been here. What have you got that the rest of us lack? And what about your sister? She was almost fighting with Joanne a short time ago about which of them was going to accompany Doctor Lindsay on his round.'

'I shall be afraid to tell Angela,' Aileen said slowly.

'You accepted his offer, didn't you?' Sally

demanded anxiously.

'Yes, I said I'd go with him.' Aileen nodded slowly.

'Well, wonders never cease! I wonder what's suddenly made him a little more human? To tell you the truth I have noticed a change in him since your arrival. Aileen, he might be falling in love with you!'

'Sally, you're being ridiculous!' Aileen could not prevent a sudden rush of emotion to her heart. There was a pounding in her ears as her blood surged madly through her veins. Was she feeling a sudden hope that the girl's words were true? She felt that she wanted to get away on her own for a few moments in order to think about this surprising development. She had never been really in love with anyone herself, and didn't know what it could be like, although she had imagination and had used it. But she felt that the symptoms now crowding in upon her were of the real malady, and to her further surprise she discovered that she hoped it could be true...

CHAPTER FOUR

Having told Sally about John Lindsay's invitation, Aileen felt easier as she went to face her sister. During the past week she had heard Angela talking about John, but only because he was the only available male within arm's length. Angela had spent some of her time talking with Pat Carmell, the porter, but Pat, although tall and heavily built and a real man's man by any girl's standard, was not quite the type Angela was accustomed to. So Angela had started talking herself into the frame of mind that was so necessary to her. She wanted John Lindsay to take notice of her. Aileen remembered this as she went to find her sister, for Angela never made any secret of her innermost thoughts. The girl was irrepressible!

Joanne Gould came out of the office, and there were signs on the girl's fleshy face that she had been crying. Aileen felt sorry for her. Joanne was quiet and aloof, and it was obvious that she was attracted to John Lindsay, like the rest of the female staff. But there was a shiftiness about this girl that did not appeal to Aileen. She could recognise it, and although Joanne was friendly on the surface, Aileen could sense that the girl held herself remote in her mind.

'Where's Angela, Joanne?' Aileen demanded.

'Gone to her room,' the girl sniffed.

'What was the trouble about?'

'How do I know? Who can say what motives your sister has? It was my turn to accompany Doctor Lindsay. But because your father is one of the pillars of this place that makes you and your sister special.'

'That's not true, Joanne, and you know it,' Aileen said firmly. 'Father wouldn't like to hear you say that. He shows neither of us any favours, and if you're honest you'll admit it. I haven't any quarrel with you. What you do or say to Angela is none of my affair. You can be friendly with me, can't you?'

'I don't want to be friendly with anyone,' the girl retorted angrily. 'All I want is to be left alone to do my work. This was a nice place before you and Angela arrived.'

Aileen sighed as the girl flounced past her and went along the corridor. She stared after the plump figure, knowing that Joanne's jealousy was at the bottom of the girl's emotions. There was nothing anyone could do about Joanne until the girl herself controlled her rebellious feelings. But it wasn't right that the girl should delude herself about the favours given out to the nurses. They were all treated the same. If anything, Robert Waring was a trifle harder upon his own flesh and blood.

Aileen went into the office, and stopped short on the threshold. Sister Preston was seated at the battered old desk in the corner, and the older woman's dark eyes lifted from her paperwork to study Aileen's flushed face.

'So you accompanied Doctor Lindsay this morning,' the Sister said firmly. 'In future I'm going to make sure I'm with him, and that will stop all this silly bickering that's going on between you nurses.'

'I'm not the bickering type, Sister,' Aileen said coolly.

'That's true.' Sister Preston suppressed the glint that came to her eyes. 'But we can't say the same for your sister, can we?'

'I'm sure you've taken that up with her, Sister,' Aileen retorted.

'I have, I'm pleased to say. I won't have that sort of thing here. This is a convalescent home, not a general hospital. The patients we cater for are charged stiff fees, and they are entitled to the best. Being daughters of our senior doctor, I would have thought you and Angela would realise that more than the other girls. But Angela is acting like a fish-wife. If it got to the ears of your father he would take a very serious view of it, I can tell you.'

'Why has Angela gone to her room?' Aileen asked.

'Because I've transferred her to night duties, starting with tonight,' came the harsh retort. 'She can't get along with Nurse Gould, and as Nurse Gould has been on the staff for some considerable time I'm taking her part in this. I hope the long hours will make your sister see sense.'

'I hope so, too,' Aileen said. 'I certainly don't like an atmosphere to work in.'

'You can start taking the patients out into the gardens,' Sister Preston said, getting to her feet. 'Mr Raynor won't be going out today. Professor Burchell is coming to see him this afternoon, and we want to prepare him for some treatment. Ensure that Miss Anderson and Mr Firth are not placed within earshot of one another, will you? They're like cat and dog. Mr Firth is an actor and writer, and he can never agree with Miss Anderson's views on the theatre.'

'I've heard some of their altercations,' Aileen said, turning to leave. She went about her duties resolutely, half her mind on the patients and the other half concerning itself with John Lindsay and her sister Angela.

When she went off duty for lunch Aileen went to Angela's room, and found her sister at the window, staring moodily out across the lawns. Angela turned as the door opened, and Aileen was shocked by the expression of discontent showing upon her sister's face. Angela was pouting, always a bad sign, and the girl's blue eyes were filled with angry storm that was fighting against suppression.

'You're a nice one,' Angela said abruptly, and Aileen entered the room and closed the door behind her. 'There I was trying to get the upper hand over Joanne and you sneaked off with Doctor Lindsay. Whose side are you on, may I ask?'

'Certainly not yours when you act like a spoiled schoolgirl,' Aileen replied. 'And I didn't sneak off with Doctor Lindsay, as you put it. He heard the row going on and told me to accompany him.'

'I've been placed on night duty.' Angela's full lips trembled. 'You know I detest it, Aileen. Won't you change with me? No one need know. You can pretend to be me.'

'No. I've helped you out too many times in the past, Angela. This time you've got night duty as punishment for that disgraceful behaviour in the office. I think you deserve this, and I hope Sister Preston makes it hot for you. We should conduct ourselves even more professionally than the other nurses, bearing in mind Father's position here, but you went to the other extreme, and it isn't good enough, Angela.'

'I'm bored here,' the girl said sullenly, turning back to the window, and Aileen saw the stubborn set of her shoulders, realising that the crisis was on its way much sooner than she had anticipated. 'I think I'll tell Father that when the six months period is up I want to leave and return to London.'

'That would break his heart, and you know it,' Aileen said.

'He's got to face up to facts. I'm not going to stay buried here for the rest of my life. I don't know what you've got in mind for your future, Aileen, but you can please yourself. It's bad enough having to live out here in the wilds, but it's made worse by Joanne Gould and Sister Preston. The terrible twins! Joanne is as jealous as hell because we're here and Father is the senior doctor, and I'm inclined to believe that Sister Preston is suffering from the same complaint. How narrow-minded can people get?'

'You haven't helped the atmosphere by doing your best,' Aileen accused. 'Why don't you think of Father's reputation? He has a lot more to lose than the both of us put together.'

'It wouldn't be so bad if I could attract John Lindsay,' Angela said musingly.

'You can forget about John,' Aileen said bluntly. 'He's not interested in you, Angela.'

'Really?' The girl looked surprised. 'And did he tell you that?'

'He did.' Aileen sighed. 'He asked me to go out with him this evening.'

'What?' Angela lost her mask, and for a moment her pale eyes glittered as she stared at Aileen. 'You didn't accept, did you?'

'Why shouldn't I? Do you think I'm not human? Don't you think I need some relaxation, too? Just because it's always been Angela first in our lives don't get the impression that I'm not human. You're too selfish, Angela, and it's about time you outgrew it.'

Angela was too shocked to say anything. She stared at Aileen, her mouth open, her eyes wide in surprise. Then she moistened her lips and her features changed expression.

Her eyes seemed to darken and narrow as she drew a sharp breath.

'So that's the kind of sister you are! You knew I was interested in John Lindsay, and you've gone out of your way to get in first. All this talk about thinking of Father is eyewash! You're a deep one, Aileen. I wouldn't have thought my own sister could turn on me.'

'Now you're talking nonsense!' Aileen was angry. 'You've always acted like a child, Angela. You seem to think you have a cross to bear. Well, I'm just as human as you, and I get fed up also. I'm utterly tired of trying to cover for you. If you're not able to stand up on your own two feet then you'll have to do the other thing.'

'Thank you very much! After all this training and studying! This is the way you say thanks to me. It was your idea in the first place to come here with Father. I don't suppose he would have dreamed of it if you hadn't put the idea into his head. Well, I'll show you exactly what I think of everything. I'm seeing Father and telling him that I don't like it here, and the sooner I get out of it the better.'

Angela walked to the door and opened it. She paused in the doorway and glared at

Aileen, who stepped forward frantically, lifting an appealing hand. But Angela hardened her expression and departed, slamming the door at her back. Her footsteps sounded quick and sharp as she hurried away along the corridor. Aileen sighed heavily and let her shoulders slump as she walked to the window.

So it had come out! She stared from the window, her eyes glittering as her mind worked over what had been said. Now she was sorry for her outburst, but Angela had come to the point of believing that everything had to be arranged for her own sweet benefit. Aileen knew she was partly to blame for the situation because she had always given in to Angela. But not any more, she told herself firmly. Even if her father had to be hurt by Angela's dislike of the home.

But it wasn't her father she was thinking about! The knowledge seeped into Aileen's mind like some insidious poison. She respected her father and loved him, and it was natural that she should want to protect him from worry. But it wasn't until now that she had stood up to Angela and told the girl a few home truths, and she realised that the obscure reason behind her outburst was the fear that Angela would try to conquer John

Lindsay. She lifted her hands to her burning cheeks as the full import of that knowledge struck her. But she was trying to read the implications beneath her motive. Was John Lindsay more important to her than her father? Aileen pictured his handsome face, and her heart seemed to lurch sickeningly. There was something about him that got under her defences. He had said the same thing about her, she recalled, and a smile came to her lips. Whatever it was that attracted her, it was mutual, and she breathed deeply as she tried to contain the new impressions flooding her mind.

She went back on duty that afternoon with her mind loaded down with worry, and it was a relief that Sister Preston did not show herself. The Sister's cool manner had made Aileen cringe, and she suspected that the same flames of jealousy burned in both Sister Preston and Joanne Gould.

The afternoon was pleasantly warm, and Aileen attended to the wants of those patients out on the lawns. She had instructions to keep a special eye on Cora Anderson and Charles Firth, and found them both interesting to talk to. Firth was not an old man, and spoke in a loud, booming voice that was reminiscent of the old Shakespearean actors. He was in his early forties, a medium-sized man with ample proportions, and the serious illness from which he was now recovering had not dampened the fire in his brown eyes.

Cora Anderson was a nuisance patient. She was always wanting something from her room, or demanded aspirin for a bad head. It didn't take Aileen long to recognise the type, but each small desire had to be gratified or the woman moaned and complained all afternoon.

By the time Aileen was ready to go off duty her heart was filled with anticipation. There was a nervous constriction in her throat at the thought of seeing John Lindsay that evening, and she knew she would not be able to eat her meal as she went along to the staff dining room. She sat with Sally Collins, and they chatted cheerfully, for Sally, having recovered from the shock of learning about Aileen's date with the man they all loved, did not blame Aileen for John Lindsay's choice. But Joanne Gould sat alone at a nearby table, deep in thought and with a tense expression upon her rather plump face. Aileen felt sorry for the girl, and glanced often in her direction, but Joanne finished her meal and departed silently, intent upon her own deep thoughts.

'What does Angela think about going on duty tonight?' Sally demanded as they prepared to leave the dining room.

'Not much, I'm afraid,' Aileen replied. 'I'd better call her now and see if she wants tea. No doubt she's been sleeping this afternoon. But she should have had more sense this morning. She knows Sister Preston isn't one to take liberties with.'

'I think you've got an enemy there, Aileen,' Sally warned. 'There's more to Sister Preston than shows. Don't get on the wrong side of her if you can help it.'

'I'm not likely to do that,' Aileen said with a short laugh. 'I do my duties properly. What more can I do?'

'You just bear in mind what I say,' the nurse retorted, and they parted on the top landing and Aileen walked slowly along to her room.

Pausing in her doorway, Aileen glanced at Angela's door. There was no sound from the room and she wondered if her sister was still asleep. Suppressing a sigh at the memory of the harsh words she had spoken to Angela, Aileen went along to the room and opened the door gently. Peering into the room, she was surprised to see that Angela was not there, and the bed didn't appear to have been slept in. Aileen went right into the room and looked around. She found her sister's smartest dress gone from the wardrobe, and two uniforms hung in a cupboard.

Had Angela gone out? Aileen turned and went back to her own room. She hoped Angela would not try any of her nonsense here. While they had been at the general hospital it hadn't mattered so much, but with their father on the same staff Angela would find it difficult to keep word of her exploits from his ears. She entered her room, and saw immediately the sheet of paper lying on her pillow. Her heart seemed to miss a beat as she hurried to snatch it up. As she thought, it was a note written by Angela.

'Dear righteous Sis,' Aileen read with wide eyes, 'I am utterly sick of this place and I'm going out for a long drive. I'm due on duty at nine, and I shall endeavour to return by then. If I don't make it then you can stand in for me. Don't think that you won't, because I know you. You'll do anything to keep Father happy.'

The note was not signed, but Aileen knew Angela's handwriting, and a long sigh escaped her as she sank down upon the bed. So it was happening despite anything she could do to avert it. Aileen shook her head slowly. What was the use of trying to maintain peace? Angela didn't care a damn about anything but her own selfishness. It had been apparent for a very long time. Now it seemed that Aileen had been wasting her time in trying to keep her sister on the right road. Angela seemed determined to ruin her career, and this was the surest way of doing it.

But she could stand in for Angela and no one need know. She knew it was a desperate measure, but Aileen was suddenly desperate. Then she thought of her date with John Lindsay and a bitter sigh escaped her. She couldn't go out with John and stand in for her sister at the same time. Could she postpone the date? It would be easy for her to formulate some excuse, and it seemed the only thing to do. Angela's position here was more important than her own hopes for romance. She clenched her teeth as she went out into the corridor to the telephone and called the doctor's quarters. She didn't like to lie, but it would prevent Angela's lapse from being discovered.

'John Lindsay!' The sound of the strong voice sent a shiver along Aileen's spine.

'This is Aileen Waring,' she replied. 'I am

most terribly sorry but I'm afraid we'll have to cancel our date for this evening.' She breathed deeply as she spoke, and disappointment was large inside her.

'Oh!' There was a wealth of disappointment in that single word. 'Is anything wrong?'

'I've developed a raging headache,' Aileen said, hoping the excuse didn't sound as lame as it seemed to her. 'It would have to strike tonight, but I'd be very poor company like this. I shall have to take some aspirin and lie down.'

'I am sorry to hear that,' he said. 'I expect you're worrying over your sister. Don't worry about our date, so long as we can renew it some other time.'

'Oh yes!' she said eagerly. 'Any time you like.'

'That's all right. You take your dope and go to bed. I'll do some work on a paper I'm writing. We'll take in that show another evening.'

'Thank you,' Aileen said slowly. 'You're very kind.'

She stifled a sigh of regret as she hung up, and went back into her room to stand at the window and stare out at the lawns. Why did Angela have to be so unreasonable? A perfectly good evening had been ruined, and on top of that she faced the prospect of performing a night duty without having had the benefit of a sleep during the afternoon. But what really worried her was having to cancel her date, and she narrowed her eyes thoughtfully as she wondered if that had been Angela's intention.

There was no limit to Angela's cunning trickery to get what she wanted, Aileen knew. Angela was aware that Aileen would stand in for her tonight, no matter what happened. That had always been the case. Aileen had always been there to do the dirty work or help out, and nothing would ever change that, to Angela's reckoning.

Aileen felt restless. She paced up and down the room and wondered where her sister had gone. Would Angela return in time to do her duty, or would she stay out and force her sister to stand in for her? As time went by Aileen was tempted to report to her father and tell him exactly what the situation was. But he would be badly shocked by this insight into Angela's character, and Aileen didn't have the heart to hurt him. She felt distressed when she realised that Angela knew this perfectly well and was willing to exploit it.

The evening dragged by, and Aileen suppressed all thoughts of what she might have been doing with John Lindsay. It wouldn't pay to start feeling sorry for herself because she had only herself to blame for this situation. She went into Angela's room, intending to put on one of her sister's uniforms. She had to become Angela for a few hours, and it must appear that Aileen was either in bed or out for the evening.

As she was dressing in Angela's room there was a tap at the door, and for a moment Aileen stood transfixed. Then she took a deep breath and went in answer. Opening the door slightly, she saw Night Sister Pedrick standing there.

'Nurse Waring,' the Sister said cheerfully, 'I understand that you're coming on duty with me tonight. I shall expect you in the downstairs office at five minutes to nine.'

'Very well, Sister,' Aileen replied. 'I'm getting ready now.'

'Don't forget to have your supper before you come on duty,' the Sister warned as she departed.

Aileen closed the door again and heaved a sigh. Now she had committed herself and there was no turning back. She just hoped that no one would miss Aileen before she could resume her own identity. But in the back of her mind was the hope that Angela would return before it was time for the night staff to report.

The minutes ticked by, and finally Aileen could delay no longer. There was an icy feeling in her breast as she left the room and walked along the corridor. Angela had no right to do this to her. Failing to report for duty was an extremely serious and irresponsible offence, and there was no excuse for a girl of Angela's qualifications.

As she reached the top of the stairs Aileen paused and compressed her lips, for John Lindsay was coming up towards her. He paused when he saw her, peering up at her with a quizzical light in his brown eyes.

'Hello, Angela,' he said huskily. 'I was hoping to see you before you went on duty. How is Aileen? She complained of a headache.'

'I've just left her,' Aileen replied breathlessly, hardly daring to look at him. 'She's asleep now. I gave her some aspirin. I expect she'll be as right as rain in the morning.'

'Good.' There was relief in his tones as he half turned away, and Aileen went down to join him as he descended the stairs. 'You didn't take long to get into Sister Preston's black book, did you?'

'Girls will be girls,' Aileen said, forcing herself to adopt Angela's carefree manner.

'We're only young once, Doctor Lindsay.'

'Your sister doesn't subscribe to that,' he said.

'Aileen is a drag, Doctor. You don't know what it's like having a twin sister around who doesn't really share your views on anything.'

'You're really very different, aren't you?' he said.

'Very different,' Aileen echoed, mentally crossing her fingers.

'I hope you're not going to get into trouble, for your father's sake,' he went on, not looking at her, and Aileen smiled.

'That's all I get from my sister,' she retorted. 'My father is well able to withstand a shock or two. I'm not going to stay here very long.'

'Is that so? You've already made up your mind to that?'

'Well, there's no point my staying on. You're the only eligible male on the staff, and you've shown where your feelings lie. You were going to take Aileen out this evening, weren't you?'

'I would have done but for her headache,' he replied, and for a moment his eyes rested upon her face.

Aileen turned to glance back up the stairs in order not to let him get a close look at her, and then they reached the ground floor and John Lindsay excused himself and went off. Aileen stood watching him for a moment, and there was a mixture of many emotions in her breast. Then she sighed and went on to the dining room. She had successfully leaped her first hurdle! If John hadn't been able to tell that she was not Angela, then there was a good chance that she could carry through this deception.

Sister Pedrick was seated at a table with a nurse when Aileen showed herself, and the Sister motioned for Aileen to join them when she had fetched her supper. Aileen did, and was introduced to Nurse Manvers, who was a slim blonde.

'There's the three of us on duty tonight,' Sister Pedrick said. 'We have almost fifty patients to watch over so we shall be fairly busy. You know how patients are at night. Half of them can't sleep, and they all need something to drink at some time during the night. I hope we'll get along well, Nurse Waring.'

'I'm sure we shall, Sister,' Aileen replied, guessing that Sister Preston would have made a report about Angela.

'Good. So long as we understand each other. There won't be any trouble if we act like responsible nurses.'

Aileen felt Nurse Manvers' eyes upon her, and when their glances met the other nurse smiled encouragingly. Aileen began eating her supper. She was wondering what Angela was doing at this moment, and was praying that her sister would not be foolish enough to show herself as Angela while there was a chance of this deception being perceived. But there was no sign of Angela at nine, and Aileen took a long shuddering breath as she prepared to go on duty. Angela had a lot to answer for, and in the morning her sister would hear all about it.

The patients were on the ground and first floors. Nurse Manvers went up to the first floor and Aileen stayed on the ground floor, where, she had no doubt, Sister Pedrick would keep a close eye upon her. She felt tired as she made a round of the patients with the Sister, and afterwards she went to make tea in the porter's room, where an older man had taken over from Patrick Carmell. Aileen chatted with him for some time, and he proved to be an entertaining old fellow, but her mind was not upon her surroundings or her companion. She was filled with an awful feeling that Angela had gone away with the intention of not returning for some time, and if that was so then this neat little piece of deception would be all to no avail. But it was too late to worry, she must see it through whatever happened.

CHAPTER FIVE

At midnight Aileen was finding it difficult to remain awake. The remaining hours of the night duty stretched before her like a vision of torture, and she knew that by morning, when she would have to report for day duty, she would feel like death. How this would eventually end she did not know, and she grimaced tiredly when she realised that once again Angela had embroiled her in an escapade, and this time she ought to have put her foot down and reported Angela absent from duty instead of stepping into her sister's shoes. But it was too late now. For the night she was Angela Waring, and it shouldn't prove too difficult to maintain the deception.

Later the Sister sent her up to the first floor to take over while Nurse Manvers went for her break, and Aileen sat in the little office trying to prevent herself falling asleep.

She tried to enliven herself with thoughts of what the evening would have been like in John's company, but only succeeded in making herself feel thoroughly miserable. She began nodding off to sleep, and jerked upright when she heard the sound of footsteps outside in the corridor. She got to her feet and went to the door of the office, to meet Pat Carmell, the day porter.

'Shh!' He said, lifting a thick finger to his lips. 'I'll get shot if they find me up here, but I never turn down a dare, Angela, and here I am.'

Before Aileen could guess what was happening he had put his strong arms about her and pushed her back against the door. She gasped in shock, and then his mouth was pressing urgently against hers, and she struggled violently to get away from him. There was the smell of beer on his breath, and it sickened Aileen, but the shock in her mind was mostly from the sudden knowledge that Angela had dared him to come here while she was on duty.

'Let me go!' she gasped as he eased back from her to look into her face. His dark eyes were a little glazed, and she guessed that he had been drinking heavily.

'What's the matter now?' he demanded

hoarsely. 'You weren't so scared when you suggested I come and see you. We were going to be very good friends, you said.'

'I'm scared that someone might catch you up here,' Aileen said desperately. 'I'm in trouble with Sister Preston, and that's why they stuck me on night duty. Sister Pedrick is watching me, and she may come up here at any moment. You'll lose your job if she sees you.'

'I don't care. I'm in love with you, Angela, and I've only known you a week. Why won't you go out with me? I've taken around some of the other nurses.' He paused and grinned at her. 'Or have they been telling tales about me?'

'Please go!' Aileen said almost angrily. 'Nurse Manvers will be back from her break soon, and I don't want any more trouble. I'll talk to you tomorrow!'

'All right,' he said harshly. 'But don't make me run around in circles after you, Angela. I won't put up with that. I'm not one of your posh doctor friends, you know.'

'How did you get in here?' Aileen demanded, her nerves taut with worry.

'Up the fire escape outside and in through a spare room window,' he said with a laugh. 'All right, I can see you're like a cat on hot bricks. I'll be off. But give me another kiss to keep me until tomorrow.'

He took her into his arms again, and Aileen froze as he kissed her. She screwed up her eyes and tried to blot out her mind while he held her for interminable moments. Then the torture was over and he reluctantly let her go.

'See you tomorrow,' he said. 'Don't fall asleep on duty.'

He turned and went off, and Aileen felt slightly sick as she stared after him. He went to the end of the corridor and entered a room. The door had hardly closed at his back before there was the faint sound of Nurse Manvers returning. The next moment the nurse appeared at the top of the stairs, and Aileen closed her eyes as she uttered up a short prayer.

'It's your turn for a break,' Nurse Manvers said as she came up. 'Thirty minutes in the dining room. There's tea in the pot and a plate of food in the oven. Help yourself.' She sniffed suspiciously as she glanced around, and there was a frown on her face as she stared at Aileen. 'Have you been drinking?' she asked.

'Drinking?' Aileen demanded helplessly.

'I can smell beer, or spirits,' the nurse

retorted. 'You wouldn't dare, would you? Not on duty! They say you're capable of anything, but drinking is past the limit.'

'I certainly haven't been drinking,' Aileen said with some stiffness in her tones. 'Would you like to give me a blood test?'

'It's nothing to do with me,' the nurse replied with a laugh. 'It's Sister Pedrick you have to look out for. Even though Doctor Waring is your father, they're going to watch you. If some of the staff can get at you they won't hesitate to do so. You know how some females are. There's a lot of petty jealousies at large in this place, so be warned.'

'I can take care of myself,' Aileen said, pretending to be Angela and almost believing that she was. 'I'll get along to the canteen now. What time is it?'

'A quarter to one! Off you go, and report back to Sister Pedrick when you return. I'd better give Miss Anderson her second tablet now.'

Aileen left the floor and went down to the dining room. The place was deserted, and she sank wearily into a chair and lifted her hands to her face. How she would face the morning she just didn't know! A sigh gusted through her and she tried to chase the tiredness out of her mind. Angela, she thought grimly, you have a lot to answer for.

There was tea in the pot, and Aileen helped herself, pulling a face as she sipped the hot liquid. It tasted like nothing on earth at this time in the morning. She sat and dozed a little, fighting all the time against the tiredness that was enveloping her. She didn't think she would be able to get through the entire night.

When it was time for her to return to duty her eyes were almost out of focus. She left the dining room, and was walking along the rear corridor when a voice called to her. She turned quickly, and was relieved to see Angela coming towards her, wearing her uniform.

'I guessed you stood in for me when I found you not in your room,' Angela said quickly. 'You're a pet, Aileen.'

'Don't try to soft soap me, Angela, not at one-thirty in the morning. But I'm not going to argue with you. Are you taking over your duties now?'

'Of course I am. You didn't get any sleep. I slept during the afternoon. Where am I supposed to be on duty?'

'In the ground floor office. Sister Preston is there.'

'Then you get off to bed and we'll have a

talk in the morning,' Angela said airily.

'We certainly shall,' Aileen retorted, and turned and hurried away. She went to her room and undressed, leaving Angela's uniform scattered on a chair. She tumbled into bed and closed her eyes thankfully, relaxing instantly and sliding down the steep slope into heavy slumber. She blissfully lost her senses until morning...

When she first awoke Aileen lay staring tiredly at the ceiling. There was a rigid thought in her mind concerning Angela, and anger made her sit up and come fully awake. She felt dreadfully tired! Her eyes were burning in their sockets. She felt irritable and short tempered. Angela had gone too far.

As she dressed and prepared to go on duty her thoughts were harsh. But she was certain of one thing. The incidents of the previous night had brought matters to a head for her. She had carried Angela around for the last time. As from today her sister could stand on her own two feet or fall into the pit. Angela was old enough to know better. Aileen was beginning to realise that by standing in for her sister she was encouraging her to follow that weak trait instead of trying to overcome it.

There was a tap at the door just before she was ready to go for her breakfast, and Angela walked into the room, smiling happily.

'Hello, Sis,' she greeted eagerly. 'I want to thank you again for taking over my duty without being asked. You're a real life-saver!'

'For the last time, Angela,' Aileen retorted tensely. 'I told you before we arrived here that I wouldn't tolerate your usual games. It isn't fair on me or Father.'

'Don't be an old meanie! I had a wonderful time last evening. I met a gorgeous male, and he's got a good-looking brother. I made a date with him for you.'

'That was very thoughtful of you! I was doing your duty while you were out gallivanting.'

'It was a bit thick, I know,' Angela soothed, her blue eyes gleaming. 'But what are sisters for if not to help out when needed?'

'I shall remember that.' Aileen sighed, knowing that she could not change her own nature. She was too easygoing with Angela solely because she loved her sister, and nothing could change that.

'And forget that you stood in for me last night,' Angela said in suddenly grim tones. 'I promise I won't do anything like that again. But I was in a bad mood last evening, and I would have thrown up the job and everything else on the spur of the moment. Because you took over for me I'm not in any kind of hot water, and it's given me a chance to cool down. I don't want to distress Father any more than you do, Aileen. But it's easier for you. You have all the good family traits and I seem to have collected a few odd ones from somewhere.'

'All right,' Aileen said with a sigh. 'But I'm warning you, Angela, that I won't cover up for you again. This is definitely the last time. I feel like nothing on earth this morning, thanks to you. It's about time you acted your age and forgot some of your selfishness.'

'I said I'm sorry,' Angela retorted in rising tones. 'It won't happen again.' She turned and whirled away to the door. 'It's my time for sleeping,' she said as she left the room. 'I shall be going out this evening, but I'll be back in plenty of time to go on duty.'

'You'd better be,' Aileen couldn't help calling after her. 'You spoiled my evening out last night. I won't let it happen again.'

There was a trilling laugh from the corridor as Angela went to her room, and Aileen shook her head wearily and sighed. Her sister would never change. She went down to breakfast, feeling very grim inside through lack of sleep, and when she went on duty she worked with a will, intent upon ensuring that she didn't fall foul of Sister Preston. If there was some jealousy here because she and Angela were daughters of the senior doctor, then Aileen intended doing all she could to prevent room for talk. She just hoped that Angela could do the same.

Her heart warned her of her growing feelings for John Lindsay when she saw him approaching that morning, and the smile which he gave her chased out the last of her irritation.

'Good morning, Aileen,' he said cheerfully. 'How are you feeling now? That headache isn't still bothering you, is it?'

'Not now, thanks. I'm terribly sorry about last night. I hope you won't think it was just an excuse to get out of going with you.'

'There's an easy way to convince me that it wasn't,' he replied. 'Come out with me this evening.'

'I will,' she replied without hesitation. 'I was hoping you would ask me.'

'Then it's a date.' He studied her strained face for a moment. 'But you're not looking very well this morning. Did you sleep well last night?'

'Not very,' she admitted. 'But I'm feeling

quite well.' She paused, then added. 'Angela told me this morning that you were coming to see how I was last night as she was going on duty.'

'Yes. She said you were asleep so I didn't disturb you. I must say that you two are more alike than I imagined. Even your voices sound exactly the same.'

Aileen watched him with steady gaze, her pulses racing. He must never know the truth about last night, she told herself.

'Well, we are twin sisters,' she retorted with a smile.

'But I know which one I prefer. I'll see you this evening, the same arrangements as for last evening. Now I must be on my round. Sister Preston tells me she will accompany me in future, so I'm afraid our getting together during duty is out for a bit. We have Angela to thank for that.'

'She's being punished for it,' Aileen said quickly. 'She doesn't like night duty.'

He went off, smiling, and Aileen watched him go. She felt her heart lighten as she considered him. He was beginning to make his presence felt, and she knew that once she started seeing him outside of duty and getting to know him there would be no going back. She was going to fall in love with him, if she had not already started the process, and there was nothing she could do about it.

Sister Preston came out of her office, and stared sharply at Aileen, but the Sister said nothing and went to look for Doctor Lindsay. Aileen went into the kitchen, and Joanne Gould looked up from scrubbing some utensils in the big sink.

'You're a dark horse,' the girl observed, wiping her hands, and there was a strange smile on her plump face.

'What do you mean?'

'I thought it was your sister who did just as she liked and had no care for convention,' Nurse Gould pursued.

Aileen stared at the girl, her mind racing as she tried to grasp the drift of the conversation. Before she could make any reply Joanne Gould laughed again.

'I saw you in Whitebay last evening. I thought you were going out with Doctor Lindsay? Or was that just a white lie?'

'I was in bed last evening,' Aileen said without thinking. 'I had a headache.'

'I don't wonder at it, the way you were carrying on. You picked the worst man in the locality, too. Perhaps there is something in the old saying about birds of a feather.'

'You're being offensive for no reason at

all,' Aileen said. 'I told you I was in bed last evening with a headache.'

'You can say what you like. I know you well enough, and your sister's car. It couldn't have been Angela I saw because she was here on duty. You were off duty. Do you deny that you met Allan Belfield last night?'

Aileen stared at the girl for a moment, her blood running cold. She had forgotten the risks in this angle of the situation Angela had created. And then she thought of John Lindsay. It would be all right for her to admit to the nurses that she had been in town the evening before, but if John should hear about it, and especially after she had called off her date with him, then the worst possible disaster would befall her. He would want nothing at all to do with her, believing that she and Angela were exactly the same after all. She couldn't deny that she was in town because that would point the finger at Angela. But she didn't want John to think that she had lied to him and gone out in Angela's car when she was supposed to be in bed with a headache.

'I don't see that it is any of your business, Joanne,' she said slowly, adopting the tone that was more suitable to Angela's nature than her own, and she saw the girl's lips

96

tighten and her face take on a sullen expression.

'It isn't any of my business,' Nurse Gould said haughtily, and tossed her head as she stalked to the door. 'But there is such a thing as personal pride. You should remember where you work and who your father is. I'm utterly surprised by what I saw. You should be very careful around a man like Allan Belfield. He and his brother are suspect. They are not very desirous people.'

'Thank you for the character lesson,' Aileen said, and there was a sinking feeling inside her as she wondered what it was that Angela had been up to the previous evening. She sighed as she went about her work. If John should learn of the facts as they appeared then she could say goodbye to him. He wouldn't want to mix with a girl who got herself talked about by the staff.

There was a thread of worry weaving itself into a tense knot in her breast as she considered the situation. All of this was boiling up because Angela was the type of girl that she was, and Aileen knew she had helped the circumstances by being weak in her dealings with her sister. She had adopted a peace at any price attitude, and Angela, being the girl she was, had soon made capital out of it.

The thought of Pat Carmell came back to her mind, and Aileen's cheeks reddened as she recalled the way he had sneaked up to the first floor to see her. The pressure of his mouth against hers made her feel sick and angry. How dare Angela lead on a man like that? She would certainly have to speak to her sister about that side of her life. The day porter was definitely not the type of man a girl could trust, and Aileen told herself it was a good thing he had thought she was Angela.

There seemed to be a parcel of trouble building up in front of her. Aileen shook her head slowly. It was Angela's fault. Something would have to be done, and soon, before the whole situation got out of hand.

A footstep in the doorway alerted her and she spun around, to find Pat Carmell standing there, a grin on his face. His dark eyes took in her lithe figure, and Aileen did not like the expression on his face.

'I'd like to have a little talk with you,' he said. 'Angela is asleep in her room, no doubt, after being on night duty. Can you get outside at about twelve? You go to lunch then, don't you? Meet me in the greenhouse beyond the vegetable garden. It will be safe there.'

'I can't do that,' Aileen said firmly. 'What are you thinking about?'

'I'm thinking of your character,' he retorted, a grin twisting his lips, and for a moment Aileen thought that he had seen through her deception of the night before. But his next words dispelled that thought and implanted one of an even worse nature. 'You were out last evening, weren't you?' he demanded.

'Is that any of your business?' she retorted.

'I've made it my business because I want to help you,' he said, his grin widening. 'I had a telephone call from a friend in Whitebay. He was quite concerned that I talk to you. He wants me to make sure you understand the gravity of your position. If you don't keep your mouth shut there'll be a lot of trouble for you as well as him.'

'What are you talking about?' Aileen demanded, again wondering what Angela had been up to the previous night.

'You don't have to play it secretive with me,' he said, smiling, 'although Allan will be pleased to know that you're not eager to talk about him. But you meet me in the green-house about twelve and I'll go into details. It's just a precaution, you know. Although it was a stolen car you were having fun in, you were driving when the accident happened, and the report from the hospital this morning is that the cyclist is on the danger list. Need I say any more? Allan has to be careful, and I'm sure it wouldn't do to have it generally known that the senior doctor here has a daughter who ran over a cyclist while driving a car under the influence of drink.'

'I–!' Aileen stumbled over her words, and lapsed into silence, her surprise stealing her speech. She stared at him in shocked wonder, and he grinned and turned away.

'Twelve noon!' he said, 'and I'm sure we can sort this out. You and Allan both have much to lose, so don't forget to be there. It can be hushed up, so don't look so stricken.'

Aileen could only stare after him as he went away, and there was a numbing sensation in her mind that blocked all her processes of thought. She suddenly felt as if she had fallen into a nightmare from which there was no awakening, and she continued with her work instinctively, staring unseeingly ahead as she tried to imagine what Angela had done during her trip to town. But whatever had happened, her distraught imagination made it seem much worse.

CHAPTER SIX

The rest of that morning seemed endless to Aileen. Before the shock of what she had learned wore off she was like an automaton, mindless, cold inside, unable to think. But by degrees the paralysis lifted and worry set in, flooding the voids of her mind. But she could not believe what Pat Carmell had told her. Angela was not the girl to do what he had accused. She was high spirited and foolish, but not criminal, and she had not appeared the worse for liquor when she finally came on duty at about one-thirty that morning. There had to be some mistake!

Aileen would have liked to have spoken to her sister before noon, but she had no opportunity of getting away, and by the time she was free to go to lunch she was so distraught she could think of nothing but getting the whole story from the day porter.

'Aren't you coming in to lunch yet?' Sally Collins demanded as Aileen turned away from the dining room.

'No. You go on without me. I have

something to attend to before lunch,' Aileen muttered, and saw Sally give her a searching glance.

'Is something wrong?' the girl queried. 'You do look upset about something. Doctor Lindsay hasn't turned you down now, has he?'

'No, it's nothing like that.'

'Then you're still feeling under the weather,' the nurse said sympathetically. 'But it would have upset me, getting a date with a man like John Lindsay then having to call it off because of a headache.'

'Do me a favour,' Aileen said, pausing to look at the girl. 'Don't mention that I was in bed with a headache last night.'

'All right, if you wish, but why?'

'It doesn't really matter, but it would help to smooth certain matters over.' Aileen started away again, and when she glanced back Sally had gone into the dining room. She hurried out of the building and made her way around to the rear. When she reached the long greenhouse she saw Pat Carmell standing inside.

He opened the door for her, grinning widely, and Aileen suppressed a sigh as she waited for him to speak. He stared at her with genuine admiration in his dark eyes, and Aileen was filled with disgust as she recalled how he had mistaken her for Angela and kissed her.

'Well, here we are,' he said, and there was a slight trace of awkwardness in his tones. 'You got yourself into a nasty mess last night, and although Allan Belfield is my friend, I must say that he isn't the kind of man you should get involved with. But that's all beside the point. You went out with him last night and you drove that car. There was an accident, the result of which is a poor old man lying almost dead in hospital. It was on the radio this morning that the police were interested in a driver who failed to stop after the accident. That's a very serious thing. Especially if they catch up with you and find out that the reason you didn't stop was because you'd had too much to drink.'

'That's a lie!' Aileen said hotly. She was certain that Angela hadn't been drinking. Her sister had seemed steady enough when she appeared to take over her duty, and she had been composed and normal. Aileen didn't for a minute think that Angela was so callous as to drive on after knocking down a cyclist. She was a trained nurse and her instincts would have made her stop.

'I'm not going to argue about it,' Carmell

103

said firmly. 'I know what Allan told me. I know him well enough to suppose that even if you weren't driving that car Allan must have some people on hand ready to say that you did.'

'What are you getting at?' Aileen demanded. 'What's this all about?'

'You're a bright girl. You're not as sweet as your sister Angela, but you've got your wits about you. You know what the score is, don't you?'

'I haven't the faintest idea of your drift. What's on your mind?'

'It's nothing to do with me, sweetheart. All I've got to do is pass on some advice to you. Don't worry about this accident. If you do as you're told there won't be any trouble for you. I have to tell you that you're to meet Allan at his place this evening at the same time you got there last night.'

'But I can't do that!' Aileen stared at him with narrowed eyes. She was thinking of her date with John Lindsay. Because of Angela she had missed it last night, and today nothing was going to prevent her seeing him.

'Don't you think you'd better do as you're told?' he demanded, his voice suddenly filled with menace. 'You're in serious trouble and there's only one way out of it. Go along with

Allan Belfield. That's a tip from a friend. Allan can be very nasty when he likes, and I don't mind telling you that I wouldn't want to get on the wrong side of him.'

'I'd better go,' Aileen said faintly. 'We don't get long for lunch.'

'Off you go then, but remember what I've said. See Allan tonight and prove that you're a smart girl.'

Aileen left the greenhouse and hurried back into the house. There was a frown between her eyes as she went along to the dining room, and she found Sally about to leave.

'You'll have to make it fast,' the girl said. 'Are you sure there's nothing wrong, Aileen?'

'Nothing at all. I'm touched by your concern,' Aileen replied, trying to force lightness into her voice.

'All right. I'll go up and relieve Joanne. She won't like being kept waiting. See you when you come back on duty.'

Aileen nodded and fetched her lunch. She sat at a corner table and ate without appetite. Her mind was reeling under the news she had learned, and she thought of her sister asleep in her room. This time Angela had really done it! But what were they to do? She tried to think constructively, but her brain seemed unbalanced by the shock of it all, and when she got up to return to duty she still hadn't formulated any plan of action.

She passed Joanne Gould in the corridor, and there was a sneering smile on the girl's thin-lipped mouth. They passed without speaking, and Aileen was worried that Joanne might talk about the headache and the evening in bed. If Joanne had seen Angela in town, thinking she was Aileen, then there was not much chance of keeping the information from John's ears. Aileen tried to close her mind to the awful outcome of such a development. John wouldn't speak to her again as long as she lived. And what would happen if Angela really had knocked down that cyclist? Everyone would think it was Aileen who had done it. Angela must have called herself Aileen or Pat Carmell wouldn't have come to her this morning.

Aileen was appalled by the extent of the situation. She was going to get the blame for everything that had happened, and apart from losing John before she even had the chance of getting to know him, there would be trouble with the police. Only if Angela told the truth would the whole matter be settled, and then the deceit that Aileen had practised the previous night to protect her sister would come to light, and the hospital board would frown upon such behaviour. It wouldn't look good for her father, Aileen told herself with increasing worry biting deeply into her awareness.

When she reached the office she was relieved to find that Sister Preston was not there. Sally was busy checking diet sheets, and the girl looked up at Aileen's entrance.

'It's none of my business,' she said in a conspiratorial whisper, 'but I think I ought to warn you that Joanne isn't the kind of a girl to respect a confidence. Apart from the fact that you must be mad to stand up John Lindsay, you really ought to take pains to avoid being seen by people like Joanne when you're not in the place you're supposed to be.'

'Joanne told you she saw me in town last night?' Aileen demanded anxiously.

'She did, and she'll tell everyone else who might be interested. I didn't think you had it in you, Aileen. Of course, it's none of my business, but whoever the man is you've found, he must be really something for you to stand up John Lindsay. Some people have all the luck. I've been trying to attract Doctor Lindsay for months, and I wouldn't look any further than him for a date. But you haven't been here much more than a week and already you can afford to turn him down! What is it you've got that I haven't?'

'Sally, you're a decent girl!' Aileen said desperately. 'I know I can trust you to say nothing about Joanne's words. There is more to it than appears on the surface, and I wouldn't want John Lindsay to know about last night.'

'I should say you don't!' the girl exclaimed. 'Joanne said you were the worse for drink! I know Joanne is prone to exaggeration, but there must be a grain of truth in even her wildest rumours. No wonder you're not feeling yourself today, Aileen. But don't worry. It's none of my business and I shan't go shouting it around. But watch your step for your own sake, there's a good girl. I'd hate to see you get into trouble, and there's your father's position here to be considered.'

Aileen longed to tell the girl what really happened, but she knew the only way to retain even the smallest grasp upon the situation was by remaining silent. Too much had evolved from what had been intended as sisterly help, and talking about it could only add to the complication.

'Sister Preston has gone to lunch, has she?' Aileen asked.

'Yes. She'll be gone for half an hour.'

'Do you think I could slip up to my room for ten minutes?'

'If you don't make it too long. You can always say that you're feeling unwell. You don't look too good, Aileen. These nights out on the town aren't doing you any good.'

'Nights?' Aileen queried as she turned to the door. 'There was only one.' She smiled tensely and departed. 'I won't be long.'

As she hurried up to her room she told herself that she was beginning to believe that she had been out last night instead of impersonating Angela, and when she reached her quarters she went to Angela's room and opened the door gently. Her sister was asleep, breathing gently, one arm lying outside the covers, and it seemed a shame to awaken her, but Aileen set her teeth and went into the room, dropping down on the side of the bed and grasping Angela's shoulder. Her sister came awake slowly, like a swimmer fighting her way back to the surface after a particularly deep dive.

'What time is it?' Angela demanded, stuffing a yawn. 'You're not off duty yet, are you? I've got to go out before I go on duty.'

'It's still lunch time,' Aileen said severely.

'Oh Lord! Why wake me up so soon?'

'Because I must talk to you. I want to know what you were up to last night, Angela? Did you use my name?'

'Of course I did!' Angela blinked, and a cautious light appeared in her eyes. 'You were using my name here, weren't you? What's all this about? Couldn't your third degree wait until I've had my fill of sleep?'

'No.' Aileen shook her head determinedly, and tugged at her sister's shoulder as Angela turned away from her. 'Tell me about the accident last night?'

'Accident?' Angela's blue eyes opened wide, and for a moment her defences were down. 'What accident?' she demanded, her expression resuming its blankness.

'Come along, I don't have much time, and this is a very serious matter. I've always thought that one day you would go too far. What about the accident?'

'I honestly have no idea what you're talking about.' A stubborn light came into Angela's blue eyes, and Aileen sighed and shook her head.

'This is too serious for you to lie about,' she said. 'If you're not careful you're going to have to answer criminal charges.'

'What do you mean?' Nervousness infiltrated into Angela's manner.

'I'm talking about the man who was knocked off his cycle last night by the car you were driving. This man you met, Allan Belfield, I think his name is. He's an unsavoury character by all accounts. He sent a message to me by way of Pat Carmell this morning. I'm to see Belfield this evening at the same time as last night. I don't like the way Carmell spoke to me this morning, Angela. I have a feeling there's a lot of trouble coming out of this. Joanne Gould saw you last night in Belfield's company. Naturally she thinks it was me, and if John Lindsay hears about it, when I was supposed to be in bed, I mean, I shall lose any chance with him that I might have.'

'I'm sorry, Aileen,' Angela said slowly, 'but I can't do anything about this. I don't remember knocking the man off his cycle.'

'You mean to tell me you'd had too much to drink?' Aileen was appalled. 'But you looked all right when you came to relieve me!'

'That was because I'd had about a gallon of coffee at Allan's place. He was very good about it.'

'I'm sure he was. What was he doing letting you drive that car in the condition you must have been in? And why didn't he stop you at the time of the accident?'

'He said he dared not! I was drunk, Aileen. How would that have sounded in the morning papers? Think of what it would have done to Father!'

'You should have thought of that before you went off last night,' Aileen retorted. 'Angela, this is terrible. That man is on the danger list. If he dies you'll be guilty of manslaughter. And you're a nurse! What are we going to do?'

'I don't know.' Angela was sullen now, and her lips were forming an ugly pout. 'I thought about it all last night while I was on duty. Allan said the best thing to do was forget it. I wouldn't help that man now by going to the police. It was the cyclist's fault, anyway. He didn't have a rear light, or so Allan told me.'

'You shouldn't have been driving in that state,' Aileen said desperately. 'This Allan is just as guilty as you for letting you drive. Where was your car, by the way?'

'We left that in a park behind a night club. He had a stolen car and I wanted to try it. But I hadn't been drinking much, Aileen. A gin and tonic and a Bloody Mary, that's all. It shouldn't have affected me like it did.'

'You shouldn't have had anything to drink,

knowing that you had your own car with you,' Aileen said. She sighed as she shook her head. 'But what are you going to do, Angela?'

'What can I do?' the girl demanded hopelessly.

'There's only thing to do.' Aileen spoke stoutly, but with a determination she was far from feeling. 'You'll have to go to the police and tell them everything.'

'That's the last thing I shall do.'

'Angela, don't be a fool!'

'That's why I'm going to do nothing,' her sister retorted. 'I'd be a fool to make trouble for everyone concerned. How will it help that cyclist? Can you tell me that?'

'Talk sensibly, Angela. That's not the attitude to take, and you know it. I haven't the time to talk to you now, but you had better think about this during the afternoon. I'll see you when I come off duty. But I'm telling you now that I won't shut my mind to all this. You went out last night in my name. As far as that Allan Belfield knows it was Aileen he met. If it came out about the accident the police would come here for me. You were on duty as far as anyone knows. Are you going to put my future in jeopardy, Angela?'

'Let me think about it,' Angela replied harshly. 'My poor brain is swimming with panic. It was quite a shock to me, I can tell you, when Allan told me what had happened.'

'This is absurd,' Aileen snapped. 'How could you forget what happened? Do you expect me to believe that?'

'It's the truth. If you won't believe it then how can I expect the police to?' Angela thrust out her underlip, and for a moment she looked like a frightened schoolgirl. 'Think of the shock it will cause Father if I'm convicted of drunken driving, or some such crime.'

'I must go.' Aileen got determinedly to her feet. 'I can't do more than advise you, Angela. You know what I want you to do. Make a clean breast of it. It's better in the long run.'

'No. Allan was strange last night after the accident. He told me that if I said anything there would be bad trouble. You don't understand, Aileen. I had decided before I left him that he isn't nice to know, and but for this trouble with the cyclist I wouldn't have troubled to see him again. But now I've got to, can't you see? If he reports it I shall be in trouble.'

'He wants to see you this evening,' Aileen said coldly. 'Perhaps you'd better go and see him. To tell you the truth I didn't like the way Pat Carmell was talking to me. He's connected with this Allan Belfield in some way. I think there's more to this whole thing than meets the eye, Angela.'

'What do you mean?' her sister demanded.

'You go along and see him this evening,' Aileen instructed. 'I'll stand in for you until you get back. You don't have to make an evening of it. If you leave here during late afternoon you can be back before I have to get ready to go out on my date with John.'

'Aileen, I'm sorry for all this. I know it was wrong of me yesterday, and you were a good kid for standing in for me as you did. I'll see what I can do to get out of this mess, and I promise you there won't be anything like it again.'

'All right, so long as you make an effort to get straight,' Aileen retorted. 'But don't be foolish, Angela, and try and forget all about it. The police usually find the driver in cases like this. The penalty is much more severe if you don't go forward.'

Angela made no reply, but her head nodded slowly as she lay back in the bed. Aileen stared at her sister's set face for a moment, then departed. There were criss-crossing threads of worry in her mind as she went back on duty.

The afternoon was long and dreary for Aileen, and as it came to a close she realised that she could not go out to meet John Lindsay until she knew what had happened to Angela. As she was going off duty she met John, and it seemed that he had been waiting around to see her.

'You're not looking too good,' he commented. 'Not troubled by that headache now, are you?'

'No,' she said. 'But there is something else. Angela has to go into Whitebay this evening. She'll be leaving at any time now, but she doesn't know how long she'll be, so I'll have to wait around until she gets back, just in case she isn't here to go on duty when the time comes.'

'That's a bit awkward, isn't it?' he demanded.

'I'm sorry, but her trip is important or I'd tell her to put it off until another time. I hope you're not thinking that I don't want to go out with you.'

'I'm not thinking that at all,' he responded. 'But I'm beginning to wonder if this is going to be just one of those things. I hope not. I want to get to know you, Aileen. I hope Fate hasn't got you earmarked for someone else.' He smiled as he saw the tension building up in her pale eyes. 'Look, I'll wait around for you. If we don't get out until late then we'll do something else this evening and leave going to town until we do have the time.' He took hold of her shoulders, and his fingers were gentle but insistent as he gripped her. 'Don't look so worried,' he commanded. 'I can wait for you.'

'Thank you,' she told him gravely. 'This is something of an emergency.'

'I understand. I'll be in the doctors' room when you are ready to go out, so come along there and give me a shout, will you?'

Aileen promised, and he took his leave of her, smiling as he did so, and Aileen felt reassured as she went on up to her room. She felt thoroughly worn out, and dropped down on her bed to relax for a few moments. Her mind was busy with Angela's predicament, and she was no nearer finding a solution. Thinking of her sister, she pushed herself wearily to her feet and went along to Angela's room, compressing her lips when she found it deserted. Her sister had gone!

For some time Aileen stood in Angela's room, staring from the window. No matter what she thought, there could be no denying that Angela's only course was to go to the police. There would be trouble, she knew, and it would shock her father, but that was as nothing compared with the trouble that would befall Angela if her sister deliberately refrained from reporting the accident. She hoped Angela's conscience would guide the girl, but she had a sinking feeling in the pit of her stomach as she told herself that Angela would dodge the issue if she could, and it hardened Aileen's own determination to make her sister do the right thing. It was going to be a difficult period for all of them, she knew, but they had no choice but to do their duty.

CHAPTER SEVEN

Aileen never wanted to face a similar evening again. The time seemed to drag and there was nothing to prevent her from falling into an abyss of worry and fear. By seven-thirty she began to despair of Angela ever returning, and she knew John would be getting impatient, and rightly so. But she stuck it out in her room, sitting on the bed and staring into space as she waited out the dragging minutes.

When there was a tap at the door Aileen leaped to her feet and ran in answer, and received something of a shock when she found her father standing outside. He smiled benignly as he looked at her.

'Hello, Father,' Aileen said, forming a smile. 'This is a surprise.'

'And a great pleasure,' he said, entering the room as she stepped back to admit him. 'I haven't had a lot of time for you and Angela since you arrived. For years I told myself that when my daughters arrived I would spend all the time in the world with them.'

'But you're very busy, Father,' Aileen said.

'Too busy, my dear.' He watched her face closely, his blue eyes almost as pale as her own. 'Where's Angela? She's on night duty, isn't she?'

'Yes. She's gone into town on an errand, and that's why I'm staying in. If she doesn't get back on time I shall have to stand in for her.'

'I'm glad that you two help each other out,' he said, sitting down on a chair by the window. 'How are you settling in, Aileen? Do you like it here?'

'Very much, Father. This was worth the waiting for.'

'That's how I feel about it.' He was smiling. 'You two girls are a great credit to me. I sometimes find it very difficult to believe that you're both here as nurses. But we must find more time for getting together. Are you making friends with the other nurses?'

'We are settling in well.' Aileen smiled as she considered making friends with Joanne Gould. That would be a full-time job, she thought remotely. 'We're well into our second week now. It's surprising how the time passes.'

'True, and you'll realise that still more when you get a few more years upon your shoulders. But that isn't why I came to see you. John tells me he's going to take you out. I'd like to talk to you about John. He's a very fine doctor and a good man, and you won't be able to do better for yourself.' He held up a hand as Aileen showed that she was going to speak. 'I know,' he laughed. 'You think I should mind my own business about this side of your life. But I'm your father, and in the absence of your mother I have to do some plain talking.'

'Father, spare me that,' she replied with a smile. 'I know how you feel about us. You're afraid that we shall make mistakes, and that somehow we'll do all the wrong things, but I assure you everything will work out for us. You just stand by and watch. We shan't let you down.'

'It's very satisfying to hear you say that,' he replied. 'But I wasn't going to talk to you in that manner. You've been fending for yourselves now for quite a long time, and if you haven't learned the lessons of life by now then it's too late for me to start in trying to teach you. All I wanted to say was that if you're going to have an interest in John then don't trifle with his affections. Perhaps it's none of my business and I ought to stay in the background, but I feel you are responsible enough to hear me out, Aileen. I wouldn't dream of talking to Angela like this, but you're different.'

'What about John?' she demanded.

'No doubt he'll tell you in his own sweet time,' her father hedged, 'but I feel that you should know because he may leave it too late.'

'What are you getting at, Father?'

'Oh, it's nothing serious.' He laughed as he took in her expression. 'He didn't have leprosy as a child, and he doesn't come from a long line of village idiots. But he is a sensitive man. I know, I've got to know him pretty well in the time that he's been here. He was engaged to be married once, and she let him down very badly. It happened just before he came here, in fact he came here because he needed the change and the chance to forget. That's not common knowledge around here, so keep it to yourself. Just treat him as a normal human being, and remember his painful experience if he seems a little moody at times or difficult to get along with. As I've said, it's none of my business, but if you get to like him a lot it would be a pity if his manner put you off.'

'That's very considerate of you, Father,' Aileen replied with a smile. 'But you needn't worry. I'm sure I shall get along very well with John.'

'I hope so. I would like to have him as a son-in-law.' Robert Waring got to his feet and paced the room. 'I'm a bit premature, I know, but time gets away so very fast. I sometimes find it hard to believe that I'm fifty-six next birthday. I've less than ten years left to retiring age. Yet it doesn't seem all that long ago when I was a young doctor and had just met your mother.' His eyes turned dreamy, and his face showed tenderness. 'I wish she could have lived to see how her twin daughters turned out, Aileen. She would have been very proud.'

'I know she would, Father.' Aileen crossed to his side, her eyes shining. But there was a dark pit in her mind that seemed to gape wider and wider as she thought of Angela. What a dreadful shock it would be for her father if that cyclist died and Angela found herself facing a manslaughter charge! She suppressed a shudder and prayed that it would all come right.

'We none of us know what's lying ahead,' he said wearily. 'But at least one of us was spared to see you and Angela grow to adulthood. Now I must be on my way. I've got a meeting to attend in Hartford. Enjoy yourself this evening. I'm sure you and John are well suited.'

'You sound like a potential matchmaker,' she accused cheerily, and he smiled benignly as he kissed her cheek and departed.

When her father had gone Aileen lost her cheerfulness. She worried more than ever over the situation, knowing how much it would affect her father's life. No matter the cost, she thought desperately, this business would have to be settled without trouble.

At eight she began to get worried. Angela

ought to have returned by now. And in the back of her mind was the concern she was feeling for keeping John waiting for her. Nothing was ever simple, she thought, pacing the room, and it had always been the selfish actions of Angela that caused the trouble.

When she finally heard the sound of footsteps in the corridor she felt weak with relief, and hurried to the door, opening it in time to see Angela going into her own room.

'Angela,' she cried. 'Where have you been?'

'You know perfectly well,' came the moody retort. 'I've had the hell of a time.'

'What happened?' Aileen entered the room and closed the door at her back. She stared at her sister, sensing that things had not gone as she had hoped. Angela was in a fury, and began taking off her scarlet dress and putting on her uniform. 'Well?' Aileen demanded when her sister made no effort to speak.

'You'd better forget all you've learned about last night,' Angela said strongly. 'Leave it to me. It's none of your business, anyway.'

'Angela, that's not the way to talk.' Aileen was appalled by her sister's attitude. 'What did happen this evening? Did you see Allan Belfield?'

'Of course I did. Just leave me alone,

Aileen. If you are going out with John Lindsay this evening you'd better get a move on. I'm back now and I'm going on duty shortly. You are just wasting your time now.'

Aileen stared at her sister, her mind refusing to believe what she heard. But she knew Angela well enough to read the expression now showing on her sister's face, and she drew a quick breath as she wondered what to do.

'It is my business that you are a hit-and-run driver,' she said grimly. 'It's a crime to withhold evidence from the police. I know about the accident and I should report it myself. I implore you to reconsider, Angela. It will be in your favour if you go to the police voluntarily. Don't leave it too late.'

'It is too late,' came the sharp retort. 'That cyclist died in hospital this afternoon.'

Aileen stared at her sister's hard face, and the worst possible despair flooded her mind. She closed her eyes as she saw disaster crowding in upon them.

'Angela,' she said in shocked tones. 'Whatever can you do now? What will happen to you?'

'Nothing,' came the swift reply, 'because I'm not going to be an utter fool and give myself up. The man is dead, so nothing I do, or don't do, will harm him. It's over as far as I'm concerned. That's why I tell you to forget it, Aileen.'

'But I can't,' Aileen said wearily. 'I've got a conscience, if you haven't.'

'Don't be so foolish, sister,' Angela replied, shaking her head. 'You've always been telling me how I have to do my best for Father's sake. So now you want me to knock him for six with this trouble! Even I wouldn't want to do that, and I'm the one supposed not to have any thought for anyone.' She sighed heavily. 'I don't like this situation any more than you do. But there's no need to make trouble for Father. That cyclist is dead. My going to the police won't bring him back to life. The least said soonest mended!'

'I've never imagined you to be anything but selfish, Angela.' Aileen spoke in harsh tones, and her eyes were bright with anger. 'But I never looked upon you as criminally without conscience.'

'It isn't like that at all,' Angela retorted, talking with the kind of tones one used with a tiny child. 'I'm scared and worried up to my neck. I can't see any way out of this except maintaining a silence. I won't help that dead man by giving myself away to the police. Can't you see that it would only heap grief and worry upon all of us?'

Angela finished dressing, and tugged a comb through her blonde hair. Aileen watched her sister as if she were a stranger, and there was a wild thought inside her that this was all part of some dreadful nightmare. But there could be no awakening! Nothing could alter the indisputable facts. Angela was guilty of a serious crime and would have to answer for it. Anything less than reporting to the police could not be accepted. But there was a picture of her father's face in Aileen's mind as she watched Angela putting the finishing touches to her make-up. What would the revelations do to her father?

'I'm going down to supper now,' Angela said. 'Please don't upset yourself, Aileen. I know it looks bad, but I'm going to do what I feel is right. It will bring the least trouble to all of us.'

'You know it looks bad!' Aileen said. 'A man lost his life through your criminal negligence and you think it's bad.'

'He was partly to blame for the accident,' Angela defended. 'His rear light was not working.'

'You can't even remember knocking him down,' Aileen said tonelessly. 'What sort of a defence will you put up in court?'

'It will never come to court.' Angela sounded frightened as she spoke. 'Don't forget that I'm not the only one involved. Allan Belfield won't take any risks. You'd better forget all this as I told you. It doesn't concern you, anyway.'

'Doesn't it? You were using my name, weren't you? As far as Allan Belfield is concerned it was Aileen Waring whom he met. Everyone here thinks that it was you on duty. I was supposed to be in bed with a headache. That was the story I gave John, but Joanne Gould saw you out last evening and naturally assumed that it was me. I'm the one likely to end up in court, and facing a much graver charge because you haven't the guts to own up to what you did.'

'Let's talk about this in the morning, Aileen,' Angela said desperately. 'I'm late now, and you have John to see. Go out with him and enjoy yourself. Forget about all of this.'

'How am I ever going to forget that my sister killed a man on the road and dared not face the consequences?' Aileen demanded.

'Oh God! I wish you wouldn't make it sound like that! It didn't happen that way.'

'No matter which way it happened, that

man is now dead!'

They stood staring at one another for several moments. Then Angela sighed and walked around Aileen. She did not look at her sister as she opened the door.

'I've got to go on duty now,' she said. 'I'll see you in the morning, Aileen.'

Aileen nodded coldly, and remained motionless while Angela departed. She listened to the quick sound of her sister's feet receding in the corridor, and a shudder passed through her. She felt cold inside, filled with an unnatural horror. None of this could be real! The thought was vibrant in her mind. It had to be part of a nightmare!

She went slowly into her own room and checked her face and touched her hair before taking her handbag and going down to the doctors' room to let John know she could now go out. She tried to put on a happy expression, but her thoughts were too grave, and she was frightened of the outcome to what could only be a bad mistake on Angela's part.

John was in the room when she tapped at the door, and he threw aside the newspaper he was reading and sprang to his feet when he saw her. A grin appeared on his face, and Aileen was apologetic as he came quickly towards her.

'I am sorry you've been kept waiting,' she said quickly. 'Angela didn't get back until a few moments ago.'

'Not to worry,' he said, eyeing her closely, and she felt a spark of pleasure when she saw the admiration in his gaze. 'I am doing better than last night, aren't I? At least we'll get a couple of hours together.' He glanced at his watch and pulled a wry face. 'Shall we go for a drive?'

'That sounds nice,' Aileen told him quietly. 'I'm sorry it's too late for almost anything else.'

'I'm not complaining,' he retorted. 'Come on, and I'll prove to you that I'm a much better driver than your sister.'

'Angela?' she demanded, and there was a suffocating squeeze of muscles in her throat.

'She didn't see those no entry signs, did she?' he demanded with a smile.

'That's true.' Aileen tried to steady her ruffled nerves. She was feeling worse than Angela about the whole matter, and somehow she longed to be able to tell John about it, to ask his advice. But she knew that was out of the question. There was no advice needed. Angela ought to go to the police and admit that she was responsible for the accident.

They left the house and got into his car. For a moment he sat staring through the windscreen, and Aileen glanced at him. His face seemed harsh as his thoughts roved over some personal thought, and then he stirred himself and glanced at Aileen. He smiled thinly.

'This is the first time I've taken out a girl in a good many months,' he admitted.

'So I've been told by the nurses,' she replied.

'Is that a fact?' He laughed as he started the car. 'I suppose I am the subject of a good many comments. No doubt the nurses think that I'm some kind of a zombie, not wanting to take any of them out. But I have my reasons for remaining remote. I must tell you that you're the first girl to make me break a hard and fast rule I made some time ago.'

'Girl trouble?' Aileen demanded, deciding to treat the matter lightly. 'Almost everyone has that sort of trouble at one time or another.'

'True, but it hits some people a lot harder than others.' He sighed heavily. 'Where would you like to go?'

'I don't mind. I'm practically a stranger

around here. You take me where you think it's nicest.'

'It's going to be dark before you'll have the chance of seeing much,' he retorted. 'But I can start a tour now and we can complete it another evening. Do you think we shall ever be able to spend a whole evening together?'

'I'm sure of it,' she replied with a smile. 'It's just one of those things. But, as you said, we are improving. Perhaps the next time it will be all right.'

'Is Angela in some kind of trouble?' he asked as he was driving down the driveway.

'No. Why do you ask?' Aileen was aware that she spoke much too quickly, and John glanced at her, their eyes meeting for a moment. Aileen turned away to stare through a side window.

'Nothing much, but I'm a very sensitive man, and I can see that you're worried about something. The only thing you do worry about is that twin sister of yours, and she wasn't looking too happy when I saw her leaving earlier this evening.'

'Angela is always in hot water of one sort or another,' Aileen told him, trying to keep a tremor out of her tones.

'She's made a name for herself here, and this isn't the end of her first month yet. But there's nothing malicious in her, Aileen, so don't worry about it. Youth must have its fling, you know.'

'Angela had hers a long time ago,' Aileen said slowly.

'Perhaps so, but you never did.'

'How can you tell?' There was a ghost of a smile on Aileen's face as she glanced at him.

'I told you, I'm a sensitive chap. I can almost read minds at times.'

'Heavens! Then I shall have to be careful!' she exclaimed.

'You'll never have to be careful!' He nodded as if sure of himself. 'I know the kind of girl you are without having to be told.'

'And what kind is that?' she demanded breathlessly.

'My kind.' His tones were firm, and there was a gleam in his eyes as he stared at her. 'I've been waiting a long time for you to come to Fairlawns, did you know? Your father has done a lot of talking about his daughters, and from what he told me about you I just couldn't wait to meet you. Then you and Angela arrived here last month to show yourselves before coming to work here, and I knew then that I would have to get to know you better. Sometimes a man is fortunate enough to meet a girl like you. I'm doubly fortunate in the fact that I've recognised you as such. Most men fail to see that much before it's too late. But I feel I have a chance of seeing my fences before coming to them.'

Aileen said nothing, and stared around as the car sped along the wide road to the coast. There was a curious tingling sensation along her spine as she thought over his words, and she could feel the tug of his personality as time went on. He was a handsome and most attractive man, and she knew she was interested in him. How that interest would develop as she grew to know more about him she had no idea, but it was easy to see the slant of her thoughts. She was more than prepared to fall in love with him, and she told herself how pleasant it would have been if the worry of Angela didn't exist.

'We'll go into town,' he said at length. 'I'll show you the cliffs and the coast, and afterwards we can have supper somewhere before returning to Fairlawns. This is a treat for me, because I rarely bother to go out alone.'

Aileen nodded, feeling more comfortable in his company. But there was guilt in her mind about the knowledge she possessed. She knew Angela had committed a serious crime! But what should she do about it? She couldn't forget it, and she didn't think Angela meant to. Her sister was scared and worried at the moment, but when she'd had a chance to think about it she would know what to do.

That thought seemed to comfort Aileen a little, and some of the despair that was in her lifted a little. She began to feel animated, and John's proximity was having a good effect upon her nerves. This looked like the start of something important, and suddenly Aileen knew that she wanted nothing more than to get to know John.

The evening was fading as they reached town, and John drove to the sea front, parking the car on a narrow road overlooking the sea. There were a great number of people about, mostly holidaymakers, Aileen supposed, and the breeze that blew in from the sea was cool. John sighed as he switched off the engine and relaxed.

'This is more like it,' he said. 'I hope we're going to be good friends, Aileen. I like to get out now and again, but I never bother when I'm on my own.'

'Then I'll make it my business to see that you do get out more often,' she retorted with a smile, and he grinned and looked out to sea, leaving Aileen with his profile to study. She nodded slowly to herself as she watched him. There was a lot in him that she liked, and he held an attraction for her that was hard to define.

Now time seemed to race by, and before very long it was dark and Aileen knew they would soon be going back. There was an impatience in her to see him again, but she was not looking forward to tomorrow. She glanced at him, hardly able to see his face, and was surprised to find that he was watching her intently. He smiled as their eyes met, and then he leaned towards her, reaching out a long hand to touch her shoulder.

'I've been watching you for some time,' he commented. 'You are worried by something, Aileen. Is it anything I can help with?'

'It's nothing,' she replied, wishing that she could tell him. 'I've always been worried about my sister.'

'So it is Angela,' he said, nodding. 'She's old enough to take care of herself now, you know.'

'It isn't that so much,' she replied. 'I'm concerned that she may do something to upset Father. You don't know the kind of girl she is. There's no real badness in her, but she seems to find trouble in everything she does.'

'So I've noticed.' He laughed softly. 'She didn't take long to get into Sister Preston's black book. But you shouldn't worry, Aileen. She'll make out.'

His face was very close to hers in the darkness, and Aileen felt her heart start pounding. He seemed to draw her, and she could not prevent herself from leaning slightly towards him, like a piece of metal attracted towards a magnet. He muttered something that she didn't catch, and before she could ask him what he said he kissed her gently on the mouth. The next instant she was in his arms.

CHAPTER EIGHT

It seemed to Aileen that she had slipped into an enchanted world. The first touch of John's lips sent a thrill through her which she had rarely experienced with anyone else. Then the feel of his strong arms about her shoulders gave her such a strong sense of security that she didn't want him ever to release her. The silence in the car built up intensely, until it seemed to Aileen that they were in a pressure chamber. Then John released her slowly and her feelings became more settled.

'Perhaps I shouldn't have done that,' he said. 'I wouldn't want you to think me too forward.' Then he laughed. 'Perhaps I'm a bit old fashioned. Times have changed a lot recently, haven't they?'

'For the teenagers, perhaps,' Aileen replied with a laugh. 'I'm glad I'm not the only one who's a little old fashioned.'

'I like you a lot, Aileen.' There was a tension in his tones that was apparent to her, and Aileen felt a little shiver run through her. So he was feeling something, too! It was in her mind that he had been attracted to her from the moment he first saw her, and she was all too conscious that she herself had been affected at first sight. Did that sort of thing really happen? She wondered about it as she watched him, and there was a small voice inside her demanding a repeat of that first endearing kiss. 'I don't often get entangled with a girl,' he went on. 'I'm sure you're not the kind of girl who wears her heart on her sleeve. Tell me, are we going to be friends?'

'If this evening is anything to go by then I'll answer yes,' she said lightly.

He laughed and reached out to take hold of her hand. Aileen could not prevent a start as their fingers made contact, and he squeezed her hand gently, making her draw a sharp breath as he released a host of rioting emotions inside her breast. They sat very close together, and she was thinking of all the other young men she had known. None of them had ever been able to touch the depths in her, as John had just done, and she knew instinctively that he was going to prove in the near future that he was someone very special. They sat still, just holding hands, and it was as if a magic spell had been cast upon them. Time passed with no conscious thought of it in either of their heads. But eventually John stirred and glanced at his watch.

'Time to go?' she asked reluctantly.

'I'm afraid so. We could get supper at a little restaurant I know, or if you wish we could visit the Claremont Hotel. I'm afraid they will be rather busy, and I didn't book a table so we might be unlucky. Another evening I'll do everything in style, when I can be certain that nothing will stop you meeting me at the appointed time.'

'I'm sure we won't have any trouble in future,' Aileen told him.

'Good.' His laugh was warm and friendly. 'Let's go visit the little back street restaurant this evening. I have a feeling this is a very special evening, and I want to remember it with warm regard when I look back upon it.'

Aileen nodded, and he moved away and then started the car. She sat silent, watching his face in the bright light that was reflected from the headlamps as they travelled the road, and her heart was singing with happiness. She had never been in love before! More than once she had been mildly infatuated with a handsome face, but no man had aroused such feeling inside her, or made her have such romantic thoughts, despite the worry that weighed heavily upon her mind. She kept telling herself that she was fortunate to have come into contact with John Lindsay.

The little restaurant proved to be Chinese, and Aileen smiled happily as they entered. She and Angela had frequented such a restaurant in London, on the odd occasions when Angela hadn't found a boyfriend to take her out, and Aileen had come to like the exotic food. The dining room was fairly crowded, but a small Chinese waiter found a table for them. It seemed that John was well known, and Aileen found herself studying his face with great concentration. He was really a very handsome man, she told herself, and her heart seemed to swell with happiness.

During the meal John kept a light-hearted conversation going, and Aileen was sorry when it was almost time for them to go. John seemed happier than she had ever seen him. He had lost some of his stiffness, and there was a brightness in his dark eyes that sent shivers of ecstasy along her spine. Just before they prepared to leave Aileen excused herself and went to the ladies' room to repair her make-up, and as she neared the door a tall man got up from a nearby table and accosted her.

'Hello, Aileen,' he said loudly, and she caught the smell of liquor on his breath. He was swaying slightly, and Aileen stepped back from him with distaste showing on her features.

'I'm sorry, I don't know you,' she replied instantly, although she had heard him use her name. She glanced at the table from which he had come, and her heart missed a beat when she saw Pat Carmell, the day porter, seated there.

'Don't try that,' the man said sharply. 'Of course you know me. Surely our little difference of opinion hasn't put your back up!'

'Please step aside,' Aileen said quietly.

'What's the trouble?' John's voice was stern as he came up behind her.

'Trouble?' the man said. 'Who said there was any trouble? Who are you? Are you with him, Aileen?'

'Do you know this man?' John asked quietly.

'I've never seen him before in my life,' Aileen retorted.

'He knows your name!' John was watching her with narrowed brown eyes.

'He's probably met Angela,' she said desperately, 'or Pat Carmell, at his table, has told him who I am.'

John glanced at the table, and nodded when he saw the day porter. Then he looked back at the man barring Aileen's path.

'You must be mistaken,' he said. 'But this young woman does have a twin sister and it's likely that it's she you've met.'

'I know all about the sister, and she's on night shift, so I know I must be right. Don't try to play games with me, Aileen, because you know I've told you I don't like rivals.'

'And who are you?' John demanded.

'I'm Allan Belfield!'

'And I'm Doctor Lindsay,' John said. 'I work at Fairlawns, too. I'm telling you that you must have met Nurse Waring's twin sister.'

'I wouldn't dream of arguing with a doctor,' Belfield said. He was a tall and powerful man in his early thirties, with blue eyes and fair hair, and he seemed aggressive and very confident as he faced John. 'What is your name, Nurse?'

'Aileen.' There was a desperate expression on Aileen's face as she spoke. 'But you don't know me. It must have been my sister you met. Sometimes she uses my name when she's out. It isn't the first time I've been mistaken for her.'

'Something should be done about girls like you,' Belfield said. 'If I can't tell the difference between you and the girl I met then I'll bet you could fool anyone. Your name is Aileen, you said?'

'That's right.' Aileen thought it better to humour him, although some of the patrons were watching them with interest.

'Angela is on night duty, and goes on at nine,' Belfield continued. 'I was with Aileen last night until the early hours of the morning. It was well past midnight when she left me. How was it she happened to be in two places at once? Can you tell me?'

'Come along, Aileen,' John said, and took hold of her arm and started to lead her away.

'You've got bad manners, Doctor,' Belfield said. 'I'm talking to Aileen.'

'You have no manners at all,' John rapped.

Belfield took a threatening pace forward, and John let go of Aileen's arm, stepping in front of her. He faced up to the man, tall and powerful, and Belfield stared at him for a moment before smiling uneasily.

'Have it your way, Doctor, but I shall be seeing Aileen again tomorrow evening. I don't know which one you've got there, and that's the truth. But I intend finding out what is going on.'

John turned away and led Aileen towards the door. Her face was scarlet as she went out into the night, and when John closed the door upon the excited chatter of the other diners she turned to him, filled with apology.

'I am sorry, John,' she said.

'Why? It wasn't your fault. It's obvious that he knew Angela. If I'm going to get to know you in future then I shall have to get used to people mistaking you for your sister.

Come along, we'd better get back to Fairlawns. It is getting late.'

They went to the car and Aileen was silent as he drove back into the country. The darkness seemed ominous, closing in about the vehicle like a menacing thing from a nightmare. But the nightmare was real, she reflected, filled with worry, and all she hoped was that it wouldn't engulf her or her hopes for the future.

'A penny for them,' John said suddenly, and she started and shook her head, forcing a smile.

'They're not worth anything,' she replied half-heartedly. 'I was thinking about that man back there.'

'I hope I won't ever mix you and Angela so badly,' he said with a laugh, which sounded forced to Aileen's keen ears. 'But he was certainly baffled. Does Angela use your name when she's out?'

'She has done. I'm not surprised at anything she does.'

'But he said he didn't leave her until after midnight last night,' John mused, thinking back over what had been said in the restaurant. 'Angela was on duty at nine. I do know that because I spoke to her. I was coming up to your room to see how you were, that headache of yours.' His voice was growing tense as he went on, as if he was suddenly realising the true facts. 'If Angela was on duty, then who was with that man at midnight?'

'Please, John,' Aileen said thinly. 'Before you start jumping to conclusions. Let me tell you something. It wasn't Angela you spoke to on the stairs last night, it was me.' In low, taut tones, Aileen began to explain what had happened last night, although she made no mention of the accident. When she lapsed into silence John laughed harshly, and for a moment she could not tell if he was angry or not.

'Well, I'm damned!' he said at length. 'So much for my ability to tell you girls apart! You must have laughed to yourself when I failed to recognise you.'

'Not at all. I was miserable last evening,' she replied strongly. 'I hated having to deceive you, but Angela had gone and you know what would have happened if she hadn't turned up for duty. I was thinking more of my father than of Angela, I can tell you, and he was mainly the reason why I masqueraded as my sister.'

'I don't suppose it matters, come to that,' John said slowly. 'Certainly Angela was on duty, as far as it goes. I couldn't tell the difference, and I'll defy anyone else to, until we get to know you properly. Poor Aileen. You had a long tour of duty yesterday.'

'I didn't mind,' she replied. 'But I began to get worried after midnight. I thought Angela wasn't coming back at all.'

'She's a silly girl!' There was an edge to his voice. 'Do you mind if I have a word with her about it? I shan't let it go any further. But she needs a good talking to, and coming from me it might shake her a bit and make her think. It wouldn't do for any sort of trouble to arise here. This isn't a general hospital, where nurses come and go and are expected to kick up a bit. Your father has a very responsible position here, and if any scandal came along it would just about finish him.'

'That's exactly how I saw it, and that's why I did what I did,' Aileen said eagerly.

'You did right.' He took a hand off the wheel and patted her hands, which she held clasped in her lap. 'I would have done the same thing had I been faced with it. But I didn't like the look of that chap Belfield. Angela should be careful how she chooses her friends.'

'I've been telling her that for years, but

she's wilful.'

'Wayward, I'd say,' he added. 'I'll get her alone when I can and lay down the law a bit. Doctors are expected to do that, and nurses usually toe the line when they come up against it. I don't think your advice has any effect upon her, does it?'

'I'm always hoping that it will,' Aileen said with a sigh. 'But so far I've had no luck.'

They lapsed into silence, and Aileen felt a little easier. It had been worrying her that John might learn from Joanne Gould about the girl she saw in town the previous night, and John would naturally have assumed that it had been Aileen and not Angela. But that risk was averted now, and she tried to tell herself that there was now nothing to worry about; but the death of the cyclist could not be glossed over. Angela still had a decision to make over that, and if her sister chose the wrong decision then Aileen herself would be faced with a problem.

When they reached the driveway to Fairlawns John stopped the car under the trees and switched off the engine. He turned to Aileen, reaching for her, and she went eagerly into his arms. Everything faded from her mind as he kissed her, and nothing seemed to matter when his strong arms enfolded her.

'Thank you for being so very understanding,' she whispered softly as he released her.

'You're a very surprising girl,' he retorted. 'But I don't blame you for what you've done. No harm has been done. I do wish you had told me about last evening. I'm a reasonable man and I pride myself on that.'

'I'm sorry, but I was afraid you'd write me off as a loss,' she replied.

'Then you acted as you did for a very commendable reason.' He kissed her again and then started the car and continued along the driveway and skirted the house. He left the car near the rear entrance, and they walked together into the house, separating by the rear stairs. 'See you in the morning,' he said softly. 'Goodnight.'

'Goodnight.' Aileen was sure her eyes were sparkling as he kissed her again, and then he departed, and she stared after him until he turned a corner and was lost to sight. Then she went on up the stairs and hurried to her room, happy at the way the evening had gone, getting a thrill from her memories of the few fleeting hours they had spent together. Then she thought of Allan Belfield, and some of the happiness fled under the pressure of the old worries.

When she reached her room she prepared

to go to bed, tired and ready for sleep, and there was a leaping excitement inside her. The knowledge that John Lindsay liked her a lot was burning in her mind. She had never felt so happy in all her life. If only the happiness would last!

There was a tap at the door as she was getting into bed, and she called out an invitation to enter. Angela came in, looking worried, and Aileen felt some of her ecstasy fade.

'I must talk to you, Aileen,' the girl said, coming to the side of the bed. 'I've been waiting for you to come in. Allan Belfield called a little time ago. He was furious. He said he'd seen you in a restaurant.'

'I don't like your choice of friends, Angela,' Aileen said grimly.

'Well, that's neither here nor there,' the girl retorted. 'The thing is, have you told John about the accident?'

'Certainly not.'

'Didn't he want to know about last night? He must have guessed you stood in for me.'

'I explained all that to him. But what have you decided about this accident, Angela? You've had time to think about it.'

'Leave it until the morning,' her sister urged. 'I shouldn't be up here, but I had to see you before you went to sleep. I've been listening for a car to come in. Let's talk about it later.'

'It's always later for you, no matter what's to be done,' Aileen reproved. 'I don't like this situation, Angela. That man Belfield is a thoroughly bad lot, by the looks of him. I don't know what you're thinking about, getting involved with his kind. The best thing you can do is tell the police exactly what happened last night.'

'He's threatened to harm us if I do,' Angela admitted slowly.

'What?' Aileen stiffened and stared at her sister with incredulity shining in her blue eyes. 'Well, that proves it,' she continued. 'If you're not going to ring the police then I shall. We're not letting a man like Belfield browbeat us.'

'Under no circumstances will you interfere, Aileen,' Angela said tensely. 'Don't you understand the risks involved now?'

'All I understand is that the police had better know about this,' Aileen said stubbornly. 'I shall do nothing about it tonight, so you'd better spend the rest of your shift thinking about it. In the morning something will have to be done.'

'You make it all sound so easy. But have

you considered what effect this will have upon Father?'

'Don't try to use my love for Father as a weapon against me, Angela. It's worked in the past, but this time you've gone too far. Don't you realise the gravity of the situation? Even I have broken the law. I know about the accident and I've done nothing about it? Aren't you concerned about that? Don't you care that other innocent people may be involved because you can't find the courage to face up to your troubles? How much harder will it hit Father if he learns about all this the hard way?'

'It's all right for you to talk,' Angela said bitterly. 'But it isn't as simple as that. You forget it was a stolen car I was driving when the accident happened. Allan knew the owner, and we borrowed the car and went joyriding in it, returning it after the accident.'

'You fool!' Aileen was so angry she could not think clearly. 'But this makes Belfield as guilty as you. Who took the car in the first place? Whose idea was it?'

'That doesn't matter.' Angela set her lips in a stubborn pout. 'The thing is, if the owner doesn't notice the slight marks on the car, or imagines that another car scraped him while he was parked somewhere, then no one can point to me and say I was driving.'

'I won't listen to any more, Angela,' Aileen said firmly. 'The whole thing assumes more gravity with each development. This isn't the result of high spirits, so don't give me the old routine about how you were feeling bored. And using Father as a weapon won't avail you. He'll have to know about it. Why should I carry this burden?'

'I'll think it out tonight,' Angela promised. 'But you've got to realise that Allan Belfield won't stand for me going to the police. And I had to admit when he rang a short while ago that you know about the accident. I'm sure he'll do something drastic if he thinks I mean to tell the police.'

Aileen shook her head slowly, failing to see any way out of the trouble except the lawful course of informing the police. But having stolen a car for joyriding before becoming involved in a fatal accident made the whole case a very serious matter. Aileen could well imagine Angela going to prison for her foolishness. She watched the girl walking to the door, and there Angela paused to look back. There was an expression of desperation in her lovely face, and Aileen felt a momentary pang of sympathy. Then she thought of the grieving family of the dead cyclist, and she hardened her heart. There was only one course open to Angela and the girl had to face it, no matter the penalties.

'It's no use my saying that you've landed yourself in a dreadful predicament,' Aileen said. 'I've told you before that your irresponsible behaviour would one day lead you into bad trouble. Now that day is here, Angela, and the sooner you face up to it the better.'

'It's too easy for you to say that, but what happens if I go to the police and then something happens to you or Father?'

'Don't be ridiculous!' Aileen was prepared to discount any threats that might have been made by Allan Belfield. He seemed to be the kind of man who would resort to that type of behaviour if he couldn't get his own way. Naturally he wouldn't want his actions divulged to the police! He was criminally involved even if Angela had been driving at the time of the accident. 'I don't think he will make matters worse for himself by carrying out threats of that nature. He's just trying to scare you, Angela. Now you had better get back on duty before they miss you. You're in more than enough trouble as it is.'

The girl did not reply, and went out,

closing the door gently. Aileen switched off the light and lay down, finding that her tiredness was gone and that worry held her mind captive. She didn't feel like sleeping now. She sighed as she turned over, but no position seemed comfortable, and she found herself worrying over the morrow. What was going to happen? No matter what Angela did, there was a series of grave charges against her. It could not be kept from their father, and Aileen worried afresh as she sought a simple way out for Angela.

She drifted into sleep, still worrying, and tossed and turned uneasily. When a gentle hand touched her shoulder she came awake instantly, thinking it was Angela back again, but a hand came out of the darkness and clamped across her mouth, almost stifling her. Aileen struggled instinctively, but a harsh voice speaking from close by made her stop. It was Pat Carmell, the day porter.

'Just take it easy, Nurse,' he said forcefully. 'There's no need to get upset. Belfield just wants to have a talk with you. He's outside on the fire escape. Promise me you won't make any fuss and I'll let go of you.'

Aileen nodded her head, still scared, and she drew a deep breath as his hand was slowly removed from her mouth.

'What are you doing here at this time?' she demanded in low, furious tones. 'You're breaking just about every rule in the book.'

'This is more serious than a few hospital rules,' he replied. 'I don't want to get dragged into this any more than you do. But it's our hard luck that your sister works here. Belfield wants to talk to you. See him and agree to what he says. I'm on your side in this. I know what he is, though, and if you give him any trouble he'll have your life. Make no mistake about that. He's a dangerous man to cross.'

'I don't want to see him,' Aileen said doggedly. 'This is none of my business.'

'That's all he wants to impress upon you,' Carmell said. His figure was tall and menacing in the night. 'Just see him now and listen to what he tells you. There'll be no trouble if you take heed of what he says.'

'And what happens if one of the night staff happens to see you coming or going?' Aileen demanded tensely. 'This is going to sound very unpleasant to Matron or my father if word of it gets out.'

'Don't worry your head about that. I've worked here for a number of years, and I've been prowling around here on and off for most of the time. No one ever keeps alert at night. The nurses are too busy with the patients or are too tired, and the night porter always sleeps until he's needed. Now I'll call Belfield in off the fire escape. For Heaven's sake agree with anything he says. I'm giving you fair warning. I don't want to see anything happen. I like my job here, and trouble would cost all of us our positions.'

Aileen did not reply. She lay tense and stiff under the covers, her eyes narrowed to pierce the gloom. She saw Carmell's figure by the window, and then heard some whispered conversation. The next moment someone climbed into the room, and Aileen froze as the heavy figure of Allan Belfield moved towards the bed.

'I haven't got much to say to you, Nurse,' he said as he paused, and Aileen tightened her grip upon the covers and held them close to her chin. 'I've got in a rare old mix-up over you and your sister. But it's been straightened out now. Angela is the girl I know, but she used your name. She also told me earlier that you know about the accident.'

'And the fact that the car you were using was stolen,' Aileen said fearlessly.

'I hope you're not as loose-mouthed as Angela,' he said silkily, but there was an underlying hardness to his voice, and Aileen could not suppress a shudder. She had the feeling that this was all part of a nightmare, but she couldn't make herself awaken from it. 'I don't have to tell you, do I, just how serious is the trouble that your sister and I are in? Well, I'm not going to take any medicine for what happened. It was your sister's fault. She was driving. If it came out then she would get the heavier sentence. But reporting this to the police wouldn't help that old man. It would just create a lot of unnecessary trouble for all concerned. So I'm telling you to forget about it. Do I make myself clear? I'm a bad man to cross, and you had better remember that if you get any ideas about talking Angela into making a fool of herself.'

'I can tell you're a very frightened man,' Aileen said. She heard him curse softly under his breath, and clenched her teeth as he moved a step nearer the bed. But she would not show that she was afraid, and her intuition told her that he would not attempt to harm her here and now. He would only resort to threats in the hope that they would be sufficient, and she was equally certain that she would not be daunted. But she was afraid, not only for herself but for her sister and her father!

CHAPTER NINE

Belfield talked on in the same vein for several minutes, and Aileen had sense enough not to antagonise him. She was instinctively aware of the dangerous potential in him, and wanted him to leave. She knew the quickest way to get rid of him was to agree with him, and she did so.

'I assure you this is none of my business,' she said. 'I don't interfere in my sister's life. What she does is her affair, so long as she doesn't involve me. That's all I have to say about it. You've wasted your time coming here, and risked trouble by making this unauthorised visit at this time of the night. You'd better go now before you're discovered. No explanation could cover this situation if you were found here, and no doubt the whole sordid story would come out in an investigation.'

'You're a cool one, and no mistake,' he said, and there was a trace of admiration in his hard tones. 'I'm beginning to think that I did meet the wrong sister. Perhaps we can get together sometime.'

'Save your breath,' Aileen said scathingly. 'I wouldn't want to be found dead in your company.'

'Just don't try me too far,' he warned, and turned to leave.

Aileen sighed with relief as his shadow darkened the window momentarily, then vanished. She heard a series of scraping sounds, then silence returned, and glancing at the luminous hands of her watch, she saw that the time was a little after one-thirty. She sighed as she laid herself down again and tried to resume her interrupted slumbers. When she did finally sleep again she knew no more until morning.

The bright sunshine pouring in at the window did much to soothe the riot of worry in Aileen's mind as she got out of bed to prepare for duty. Pausing by the window, she stared out at the bright early morning, listening to the song of the birds in the many trees in the grounds, wondering why life had to be so difficult and hoping that the difficulty would not spread to her own personal life. Now she had so much to look forward to. With John getting to know her she was finding the perfect atmosphere after so many years of emptiness.

She smiled thinly as she tried to recapture some of the magic of the night before. John's lips against hers and his arms around her! She trembled ecstatically as the visions arose in her mind. But the dark shadows of her sister's guilty secret lay over her like a bad dream. Angela would have to do something immediately about her troubles, before they grew out of all proportion. Allan Belfield had shown himself to be a man who would take no opposition from anyone. He seemed to have only one answer to any problem, and he had shown that side of his character by his night visit.

Aileen shivered as she recalled the shadows in the night. It all seemed so unreal! But then, so must the death of the cyclist appear to his family. That thought stiffened her, and she shook her head slowly. There seemed no way out except by seeing the police. Angela had to see sense, no matter what Allan Belfield threatened.

At breakfast she sat beside Sally Collins, and the girl studied her face intently, until Aileen noticed and remarked upon it.

'I'm just wondering what it is I lack,' Sally said with a grin. 'I've been trying to impress John Lindsay ever since I've been here, but with no success. You never tried to get him, but within two weeks he's eating out of your hand. Did you enjoy yourself last evening?'

'I had a wonderful time,' Aileen replied, dragging her mind from thoughts of Angela. She had been tempted to talk to her sister, but Angela had gone to bed immediately upon coming off duty, and Aileen knew from long experience that nurses coming off night shift slept heavily during the early morning. Any interruption would spoil the chances of a long sleep during the rest of the morning and early afternoon.

'Well, tell me about it,' Sally said eagerly. 'Where did you go?'

Aileen sighed and launched herself into a description of her evening out with John. Sally listened attentively, and Aileen felt sorry for the girl as she recognised the expression on Sally's face. The girl was more than halfway to being in love with John.

Joanne Gould came into the dining room. The girl was late, Aileen thought idly, and she seemed to have spent a poor night. There was strain showing in Joanne's face, and the girl almost sneered as she looked across at their table.

'What's wrong with Joanne?' she demanded in an undertone of Sally, who glanced across at their colleague.

'She's always had a sour outlook upon life,' Sally retorted. 'Don't worry about her. She set her cap at John Lindsay soon after she arrived, but she didn't get anywhere with him. Now that you've done what we've all failed to do, she doesn't like it, and she isn't sporty enough to wish you all the best.'

'Like you're doing,' Aileen said. 'I hope I haven't upset any of your dreams, Sally.'

'Don't worry.' The girl smiled. 'If John Lindsay was ever going to mean anything to me he would have taken steps to get to know me long before you arrived at Fairlawns. It isn't on the cards, I'm afraid, but that's no reason why I should take it out on you just because your face fits in with the picture he carries around in his heart. Perhaps I looked too much like the girl he almost married.'

'You knew her?' Aileen demanded.

'Not personally. But I knew someone who did. The girl was brunette, so it lets you out. Perhaps that is why he's taken to you now. Anyway, it's a healthy sign that he hasn't tried to find someone who does look like that girl generally. Perhaps that is the reason why I lost out.'

'He seems a very nice person,' Aileen felt constrained to say. 'Whatever went wrong in his life before, I wouldn't blame him for it.'

'No. I heard this other girl was a real tartar. It's a blessing in disguise that his love affair turned out the way it did. She was not right for him. But love is like that, isn't it? It just doesn't care about some people.'

'I've always thought like that, until I arrived here,' Aileen said. She was watching Joanne Gould. The girl had taken her breakfast to a nearby table, and was eating the meal slowly, her attention obviously riveted upon what she and Sally were saying.

'Shall we go?' Sally asked, also watching Joanne. They got up to leave, and Sally paused by Joanne's table as they departed. 'I can never remember seeing you late for duty, Joanne,' she said conversationally. 'What happened? Did you oversleep?'

'No,' the girl retorted in her remote tones. 'Sister Preston knows I'll be a bit late. I made a complaint this morning and the police are here to check up on it.'

Aileen felt her blood run cold at mention of the police, and she sensed that Joanne was watching her intently. She frowned as she looked at the girl, and when their glances met Aileen saw a triumphant gleam in the other girl's eyes.

'What did you find to complain about?' Sally persisted.

'Someone was prowling around last night,' Joanne said, still watching Aileen, and there seemed to be some sort of a message in her taut features. 'We never had any trouble at all until our new staff arrived.'

'What do you mean?' Aileen demanded. 'Who was prowling around last night? I didn't see or hear anything.' She was breathing shallowly, her nerves stretched to breaking point. Had this girl really seen or heard anything last night? There was a sinking feeling in her breast. It would be too much of a coincidence to expect that the girl had either dreamed or imagined intruders.

'Then you must be a heavy sleeper,' Joanne said. 'What about you, Sally? Your room is next to mine.'

'I'm dead when I get to sleep,' the girl replied brightly. 'I wouldn't wake up if the place burned down. A fireman would have to come in and get me and carry me down a ladder.'

'Well, the police will want to question you,' Joanne said. 'If you did see or hear anything then you'd better tell about it.'

'What about the night staff?' Aileen asked casually, still trying to control her fast-beating heart. 'Did they report anything unusual?'

'Half of them are asleep most of the time,' came the sharp retort, 'and the other half are girls on whose word I wouldn't rely.'

Sally shook her head and prodded Aileen in the back. 'It's time for us to go,' she said sharply, and Aileen sighed with relief as they left the dining room.

'What do you make of that?' she demanded, facing Sally in the corridor.

'Wishful thinking, if I know Joanne,' Sally replied impishly. 'But don't pay any heed to her, Aileen. She imagines much of what happens in her life.'

'But she's called in the police, so she must have been frightened by something.'

'She likes to make a fuss about everything,' Sally said. 'We've never had any trouble around here. We're too remote for men to bother about haunting us. It's not like some places I've worked in.'

Aileen nodded and they went on duty. At first there was a period of bustle as they readied the patients for the day. But Aileen was only half occupied by her work. The inner parts of her mind were filled with worry, and there was a thin vein of longing inside her. She wanted to see John Lindsay. The worry in her mind was overshadowing the growing love in her heart, and she felt that sight of John would restore her to full confidence. Apart from that she was concerned over Joanne's story about seeing intruders during the night. If the girl had reported to the police then there would be questions asked, and that meant lying to conceal what she knew.

She felt that she was being drawn into a finely woven trap, that her attempts to get her sister out of trouble were only making matters worse, and involving her. Before long it would be too late for anyone to do anything, and nothing short of a miracle would transform the situation to its former uneventfulness.

When she went into Cora Anderson's room the actress was still asleep, and Aileen checked that the woman was all right. The actress opened her eyes and peered up at Aileen. She never had much to say for herself at this time of the day, and Aileen asked after her health, bearing in mind that it was her mental state that needed watching.

'I'm living,' came the toneless reply. 'Sometimes I'm sorry even for that.'

'That's the wrong attitude to take,' Aileen said. 'There are people with a lot more to worry about.'

'I feel sorry for them, dear, but their plight

doesn't make mine seem any easier.'

Aileen went on, and upon entering Paul Raynor's room she was confronted by the novelist. He was not very tall, but heavily built, and he seized hold of Aileen's wrists with trembling hands. She stared at him, trying to gauge his mood. Here was someone who had suffered greatly, and there seemed little hope for his recovery. Most of the time he would sit by the window, just staring into space, seeing nothing because his brain had protested against the strain of his work or the worry that had accompanied it.

'How are you this morning, Mr Raynor?' she demanded in cheerful tones, and he released his hold upon her and went to the window. He rarely spoke to the nurses, Aileen knew, and she could not help wondering if the treatment he had received would ever benefit him. Watching him, she wondered why Angela had not taken heart from the fact that there were others in the world who suffered a great deal more than average. Her sister was too selfish to make the observation, she thought, and left it at that.

Sally came along the corridor and called to her. Aileen felt her heart miss a beat as she turned to face the girl. She could tell by the expression on Sally's face that something unusual was happening.

'You're wanted at the office,' the nurse said cheerfully. 'A policeman would like to question you.'

'A policeman!' Aileen could feel the coldness striking through her. There was a clammy sensation in the pit of her stomach.

'Well, don't look so scared!' Sally declared. 'It's only about Joanne's intruders last night. The police want to know if anyone else has seen anything.'

'I must be very adolescent,' Aileen said with a laugh. 'But the mere sight of a policeman's uniform gives me the tremors.'

'A guilty conscience over something,' Sally said. 'The boys in blue are our best friends, aren't they?'

'I should think so.' Aileen nodded eagerly. 'I've almost finished along here. I'll go along to the office afterwards.'

'You'll do no such thing. I was sent to take over from you. Go along now, and if it is such an ordeal, then hurry up and get it over with.'

Aileen turned away, taking a deep, steadying breath as she walked towards the office. It wouldn't do to show any kind of emotion, she told herself grimly. Sally had

169

seen her fear, and if the policeman interpreted her expression as easily then he might guess that she was trying to conceal something. Perhaps she had been seeing too many American thriller films, but she could not shake off the feeling of impending doom as she reached the office.

Sister Preston appeared in the doorway as Aileen reached it. The Sister stared at her intently, and to Aileen's guilty mind that was significant.

'Come in,' the Sister said sharply. 'What do you know about this nonsense Joanne Gould reported?'

'Nothing at all,' Aileen said, entering the office behind the Sister and finding herself face to face with a very tall constable. His helmet lay on the Sister's desk, and he was standing in a corner, his rugged face expressionless, his eyes sharp and very blue.

'This is Nurse Aileen Waring,' Sister Preston said rather sweetly, and there was such a change in the Sister's tones that Aileen glanced sharply at her. 'She's not to be confused with Nurse Angela Waring, her twin sister who's on night duty. This is Constable Daynes from the village of Dutton just along the road from here. He'd like to ask you a few questions.'

'Certainly,' Aileen said casually, feeling that she had to say something before her throat constricted and prevented her from talking at all. 'Nurse Gould mentioned something about this when we were at breakfast. I'm afraid I can't help you, Constable. I came in last night and went to bed, and didn't hear a thing all night.'

'I see.' His large hand moved uneasily. There was no expression on his face, but Aileen could see that his keen eyes were boring into her, as if he suspected that she knew something. She smiled, hoping to allay his suspicions, although she realised that he could have none. It was her own guilty conscience that was at work.

'I don't know Nurse Gould very well, having been here only two weeks, but from what I have seen of her I'd say she has a vivid imagination.'

'That's exactly what I've told you,' Sister Preston said, and suddenly the tension was gone from Aileen and she felt at ease. 'Nurse Gould is one of those girls who never seem to go anywhere or do anything out of the ordinary. She is a busybody, I must admit, and she isn't above sneaking on her sister nurses. I'm not slandering her when I say this. I just want to give you an idea of what she's like.'

'But she's made a complaint, and she states that she actually saw a man or two men, she can't be sure which, crossing the lawn at the rear of the house.' The constable shrugged his powerful shoulders. 'We can't say that she didn't see someone, and if she did then we've got to establish that person's identity.'

'Could it have been the night porter?' Aileen asked.

'I've checked with him, obviously,' came the swift retort. 'He wasn't out at that time of the night. I've also seen the two doctors, in case one of them was up to see a patient, but they have confirmed that they were in bed at the time.'

'Have any of the other nurses said they've seen or heard anything suspicious?' Sister Preston demanded.

'No. I haven't been able to check the night staff because they're asleep. I shall have to come along tonight and have a word with them. It's a very serious matter if there is someone prowling around here after dark. You're remote here.'

'But we have some men on the premises,' Sister Preston said. 'I think we could handle anything that comes up. Is there anything else you'd like to ask Nurse Waring?'

'Not at the moment.' There was a little warmth in the tones, but Aileen shivered at the keen expression in the policeman's sharp eyes. Sister Preston spoke quickly.

'Very well, Nurse, you may go back to your duties. Would you like a cup of coffee, Constable, before you leave?'

Aileen smiled as she departed. So Sister Preston was human after all. But her smile faded as she walked back along the corridor. This was getting too much of a worry. Angela was at the root of it, but her sister was asleep in her room, not in the least worried by what had happened. It wasn't fair, Aileen thought slowly. Now more than ever she wanted a clear mind and the chance to find out exactly what her feelings were for John. But her feelings were being buried under a mountain of concern for her sister.

The morning seemed to drag then, and Aileen kept looking along the corridors for sign of John. What would he be thinking now of the events of the previous evening? Would what had happened at the restaurant, and her explanation afterwards, make any difference for the way he seemed to be taking to her? She trembled as she thought of his kisses. Her heart seemed to flutter as she recalled the strength of his arms about her. That was love! She was certain of it. Never had she been so deeply stirred. He had awakened strange emotions inside her, such as she had never thought existed in her make-up.

When John came along the corridor she didn't notice him, and her first intimation of his arrival was when he placed a hand lightly upon her shoulder. Aileen jumped almost a foot in surprise, and whirled to face him, her face softening when she saw him, and there was a brooding expression in his eyes as he greeted her.

'Your nerves are bad!' he observed. 'Are you worried about anything, Aileen?'

'Not to my knowledge.' She smiled. 'You startled me, that's all.'

'Have you seen the constable this morning?'

'Yes.' The abruptness of his question touched the guilty chord in her mind and she flushed a little, feeling confused under his eyes.

'Is there any truth in the complaint that Nurse Gould made?' His brown eyes were bright as they regarded her lovely face.

'About someone prowling around the

grounds during the night?' she queried, and shrugged. 'I don't know. I didn't hear anything after I went to bed.'

'I had a feeling that someone was trying to see you, or more likely, Angela.'

'Really?' Aileen didn't like playing games with him, despite the gravity of the moment. She longed to tell him everything, to try and wipe out the shadow of doubt in his dark eyes. But she couldn't tell him about the accident. That wouldn't be fair. She knew from her own feelings that it was a dreadful secret to have. She was suffering because she knew, and the decision that had to be made – whether or not she herself should tell the police about it – seemed impossible to solve. On the one hand there was her public duty, and the action demanded by her conscience, and on the other was the loyalty she felt towards her sister, not to think of the effect all this would have upon her father. She just could not pass all this worry to John. The strain of it might prove just too much for any love he might feel for her. Love was a delicate bloom in the mind, and loving care had to attend it right up to maturity. The slightest cold wind of disillusion could destroy it completely, and Aileen knew she didn't want to lose John.

'There is something worrying you,' he said, jerking her from her dismal thoughts. 'I told you I'm a very sensitive person, Aileen. I can almost read your thoughts. Won't you share it with me, whatever it is? I'd like to help, and I'd be only too happy to try.'

'It's nothing, John,' she said slowly. 'I've always worried about Angela. She's the kind of girl that instils worry in a sister. There's nothing you or anyone can do.'

'Is Angela in some kind of trouble?' he persisted.

'I don't think so.'

For a moment they stared at one another, and Aileen could guess at the thread of thought running through his mind. Then he smiled, and reached out to pat her shoulder.

'All right,' he said. 'I know I'm still a stranger to you, but give me time.'

Aileen wanted to protest that he had never been a stranger, but her lips remained closed, and she could only nod slowly, afraid of saying anything because she felt like breaking down and telling him all. She needed a shoulder to lean upon. He was just right for her. She knew that already, had known it from their first meeting. But she could see that he was undecided about her, and it was only because of what had happened last night. He couldn't afford to get involved in any kind of scandal, and no doubt he was wondering just what sort of daughters his senior doctor had. Aileen herself could feel deep disappointment at the way life was turning out here. She had looked forward so long to coming here, and everything was turning sour.

'I'll see you later,' he said distantly. 'Can we get together this evening?'

'Yes, if you want,' she replied hopefully, and saw him smile.

'Shall I pick you up at seven? We could take in that show I promised.'

'I'd like that very much,' she said, and held higher hopes as he left her. Perhaps there was a chance for her after all.

CHAPTER TEN

Aileen was prey to many fears throughout the rest of the day, and as late afternoon approached she began to wonder what could go wrong to spoil her evening. She intended seeing Angela before going out, and she wanted to have a long, serious talk with her sister. Matters had to be brought to a head. The police wouldn't stop looking for the car that had knocked down the cyclist, and at any time a witness might come forward with enough evidence to pinpoint the guilty driver. There were too many side issues coming from Angela's inability to face up to her actions. The consequences were likely to be serious, but that fact didn't lessen the duty Angela owed to the family of the dead man.

She and Sally Collins were taking in the patients from the gardens to prepare them for tea, and Aileen kept looking around for sight of John. She hadn't seen him all day, since he had asked her out, and she was buoying up her hopes with that hopeful sign. He wouldn't have asked her out again if he felt that she was not desirable to know. But what would happen when it became known about Angela's dreadful accident? Could anyone sympathise with a girl who failed to stop after injuring someone on the road? And wouldn't opinion be against that girl's sister in some smaller measure? She knew public opinion was a harsh judge, and she was inwardly praying that John would not conform to the natural instincts of the human in a community.

Joanne Gould was leading Paul Raynor towards the house, holding the novelist's arm. He was like a child, uncomplaining, unable to think for himself, and Aileen could not prevent a tremor of pity from sneaking through her. It was terrible that such an intelligent man should have such an affliction. His situation made her realise just how foolish she was in allowing her worries to dominate her. She drew a deep breath as she pushed the wheelchair with Miss Anderson in it along the path. Why couldn't Angela find a conscience?

She was coming from Cora Anderson's room after putting the ageing actress into bed when she heard a cry from Paul Raynor's room. It sounded like Nurse Gould, she decided, going along to investigate, and there was the sudden clatter of furniture being overturned. Reaching the door of the sick novelist's room, she peered inside the room and was shocked to see the patient grappling with Joanne Gould. The nurse was lying on the bed and Raynor had his hands at her throat.

For a moment Aileen stood frozen in shock, and then she glanced along the corridor and saw Sally coming from Charles Firth's room. Beckoning to the girl, she hurried into the room, calling firmly to Raynor as she did so.

'Come along, Mr Raynor,' she said authoritatively, grasping his elbow. 'Sit down over here and I'll get Doctor Lindsay to come and see you.'

Raynor turned swiftly, releasing Joanne, who began crying out in shock and pain. The girl's face was purple from the throttling she had experienced. Raynor seized hold of Aileen's shoulders, pushing her back across the room until she was against the wall. She spoke to him firmly, but could see there was no animation in his dark eyes. The nurses had been warned that the treatment Raynor was receiving, aimed at bringing him back to full awareness, might suddenly trigger off violence in him as the first symptom of its success. They had been expecting it to happen, but this was still a shocking experience.

Raynor was making strange little sounds in the back of his throat. His strong hands shifted suddenly from Aileen's shoulders, working up towards her throat, and she felt a moment of panic as she tried to reason with him. She caught a glimpse of Sally coming into the room, and saw the shock which came to the girl's face. Joanne Gould was still lying on the bed, gasping for breath, and she started screaming when she saw Sally.

Aileen ducked under Raynor's arms and moved behind him, trying to keep his hands from her throat. Sally crossed the room and slapped Joanne hard in the face, the sound of the slap startling Aileen, who glanced round. She dimly heard Sally telling Joanne to fetch the doctor, and in that moment, when her attention was off Paul Raynor, he whirled around and attacked her savagely, grasping her throat in his powerful hands and forcing her to her knees.

Aileen was fully occupied trying to break the grim hold, but she heard Joanne get up and run blindly from the room, A blackness swooped before her eyes as she tried vainly to break the hold upon her. The silence that accompanied the attack was more frightening than if Raynor had been raving. Then Sally joined in the struggle, and instantly Raynor released his hold of Aileen and she fell gasping to the floor.

Looking up, Aileen was surprised to see Sally holding the bigger man in a firm grip, having applied some sort of an arm-hold that made Raynor helpless, although he continued trying to break free. Sally was staring at Aileen, and there was a shadow of relief upon her face when Aileen began to get to her feet.

'I think I can hold him,' the girl said. 'I've sent for the doctor. Keep back, Aileen. I learned a lot of this stuff when I was a student nurse. One of my boyfriends was a judo instructor.'

'I wish I'd taken the trouble to learn something like that,' Aileen said in shaken tones. She went forward, talking to Raynor, trying to pacify him in the way she had been taught. Sally's face was white, grim with concentration, and Aileen had to admire the girl's determination. Their patient was a strong man who knew no limitation in this mood.

The door of the room was suddenly pushed wide, and Aileen looked around with relief flowing through her, hoping that John had arrived, but it was Pat Carmell who appeared. He came forward quickly to help in subduing the patient, and Paul Raynor was lifted bodily and placed upon the bed. It was then that he started raving, and the sounds of his voice echoed through the room.

They held Raynor down on the bed, and it needed the combined strength of the three of them to keep him there. They fought him silently, matching themselves against him, and Aileen prayed that Nurse Gould had managed to find John.

After what seemed an age John did appear in the doorway, and he hurried to the side of the bed, a hypodermic in his hand. He pushed up Raynor's sleeve and quickly injected the sedative. It acted quickly, and Raynor suddenly slumped and relaxed.

There was a sigh of general relief as they relaxed around the bed. John examined Raynor, then nodded as he straightened.

'We've been hoping for this to happen,' he said. 'But not in this way. Thank you all for rallying round so quickly. Poor Nurse Gould has collapsed in Sister's office, but I think it's due to shock more than anything. Carmell, will you check that the security room is prepared? We'll have to move Raynor in there now.'

The day porter went off quickly, but not without a sidelong glance at Aileen. Sally stood rubbing an arm, her face slowly returning to its normal colour. Aileen stood with a hand to her throat, and John removed the hand, holding it gently while he examined the bruises showing dully on her throat.

'We should have taken more care,' he said. 'But you're all right, Aileen. Sally, stay with

Raynor until I come back, will you? I'd better take a look at Nurse Gould, just in case. I think you'd better check that security room, Aileen. Tell Carmell to remove all unstable furniture.'

Aileen followed him out of the room, and went in one direction while he hurried off in the other. She found Carmell in the special room, already removing some of the furniture that was not suitable for a patient such as Raynor, and the porter paused in his work and looked up at Aileen, a thin smile coming to his rugged face.

'I've had a worrying morning,' he said without preamble.

'Not through any action of mine,' she retorted quickly.

'At first I thought you'd made a complaint about last night. But I figured you were smarter than that. Your sister has a lot at stake even if you haven't. It was that stupid Nurse Gould, wasn't it?'

'She saw or heard something, and rightly complained this morning,' Aileen retorted. 'I would have done the same thing had I been in her position. I was extremely angry with your actions last night, and I shall make a complaint myself the next time anything like it happens.'

'Don't worry, it won't happen again, I promise you,' he replied thinly. 'But when Alan Belfield says jump then a lot of people around here go through the motions. I was against his coming, I can tell you. It is a risky business, and Nurse Gould must have got a glimpse of us. But the worst is over now. I think Belfield is convinced now that you and your sister won't say anything to the police about the accident.'

'Why should he be so worried? Angela was driving the car, wasn't she?'

'That's what Belfield said!' Carmell shrugged his heavy shoulders.

'It's strange that Angela didn't remember anything about it,' Aileen mused.

'Shock, probably. You should know all about that.'

'What is Belfield so afraid of? If he wasn't responsible for the accident then he has nothing to fear. Angela would face the charge of reckless driving, or whatever it is the police would charge her with.'

'It was a stolen car, remember?' Carmell came to stand in front of Aileen, his heavy face close to hers. 'That would make him equally guilty in the eyes of the law, and he's had some trouble in the past, so he can expect a heavy sentence if he ever gets caught again.'

'If he's that afraid of getting caught then he should curb his unlawful tendencies.'

'You tell him that!' Carmell laughed harshly and turned away.

Aileen went off to fetch some linen for the bed, and as she passed the Sister's office Joanne Gould emerged, her face ashen. The girl stared at Aileen, and burst into tears. Aileen went to her side as John came out of the office.

'Take her to her room, Aileen,' he said. 'It's almost time you went off duty, isn't it?'

'Very soon,' Aileen said.

'I've given her a sedative. Just see that she gets into bed, will you?'

Aileen nodded and led the girl away. She was trembling herself, shaken by the incident. It had affected her strongly, coming on top of the worry she had, but she held herself under control, knowing that nothing would be accomplished by a show of nerves. She helped Joanne to her room and saw her safely into bed. Joanne was drowsy as Aileen left her, but she murmured her thanks, and that surprised Aileen.

Angela's door opened as Aileen closed Joanne's, and Angela appeared dressed in her smart blue dress and carrying her handbag and cardigan. Aileen frowned. There was no sign of worry in her sister's face, and she suffered a spurt of anger when she realised that she was doing all the worrying.

'Where are you going, Angela?' she demanded thinly.

'Out!' The girl sounded surprised. 'I don't go on duty until nine. That gives me several hours.'

'And where are you going?'

'Just out. A girl needs a little relaxation.'

'The sort you had the night before last when the cyclist was knocked down?'

A shadow crossed Angela's face, and her lips pouted. She looked exactly like a spoiled child, Aileen told herself, but this time there was no sympathy in her. She hadn't Angela's ability to forget.

'There's no need to talk like that,' Angela said irritably. 'What's past is past. I can't help that cyclist by making trouble for myself. I told you that before.'

'You made trouble for yourself the moment you got into that car, knowing it to be stolen,' Aileen replied. 'Go back into your room so we can have a talk. I can tell that your conscience is nonexistent. But I've been worried sick since I learned of this and something has to be done.'

'It's none of your business!' Angela said hotly.

'We've been over that before! I'm involved and you very well know it. I was accosted by your charming friend Allan Belfield last night when I was out with John, and during the night Pat Carmell brought Belfield up the fire escape and into my room. I was warned not to try and influence you into going to the police. On top of that Joanne was disturbed last night, and reported to the police that she saw someone in the grounds, prowling around. A constable was here this morning asking questions, and it's your turn to see him tonight when you go on duty.'

Angela's face had turned pale, and fear stared at Aileen from her sister's pale eyes. She smiled, all sympathy gone, washed away under a deluge of worry.

'That's made you think, hasn't it?' she demanded. 'How can Belfield help you now?'

'What happened last night has nothing to do with me!' Angela refused to go into her room, and started circling Aileen with the intention of going on her way. Aileen sighed in exasperation and took hold of her sister's shoulders, pushing the girl back into the room from which she came.

'Angela!' she cried. 'Can't you see that

you've gone over the limit this time? You haven't just pulled off some high-spirited joke. The night before last a man was knocked down by the stolen car you were driving. That man is now dead. Think, girl, for Heaven's sake! Don't let this go any further. Can't you see what it's doing to me?'

'Well, that's your fault. You've always concerned yourself in my business. Now you can leave me alone.'

'I've looked after you because you've needed it!' Aileen said angrily, her patience gone. 'If you're not going to call the police then I am.'

'I wouldn't advise that,' Pat Carmell said at their backs, and Aileen spun around in surprise. He had approached silently, and now he stood confronting them, his rugged face showing menace. But Aileen recognised the glint in his eyes. It was produced by fear. 'How many times do I have to tell you about Allan Belfield? Do you think he'll let you just inform on him like that? You might tell the police, but I'll bet that before the case comes to court something will have happened to both of you or to your father. So why don't you play safe and forget all about it? There's no need for anyone else to get hurt, is there?'

'Don't try to bluff me!' Aileen said firmly. 'I can tell that you're scared, the same as Belfield. He was afraid last night when he spoke to me. I'm beginning to think there's more to this business than meets the eye!'

'What do you mean, Aileen?' Angela demanded.

'Come into the room and talk to me,' Aileen said angrily. 'I want to know exactly what did happen the night before last.'

'I'm going into town, if your intentions are lying in that direction,' Carmell said quickly. 'Give me a lift, Angela.'

'I'll talk to you later, Aileen,' Angela said. 'I have to go now.'

Aileen put out a hand to arrest her sister's forward movement, but Carmell was quicker, and his hand grasped her wrist. He held her tightly, hurting her arm, until Angela had got out of reach. Then he released Aileen and followed her sister, keeping between them. Aileen sighed deeply as she watched them go. There was a struggle taking place in her mind. All her instincts told her to call the police and report what she knew. But she was afraid that Allan Belfield might be the kind of man they said he was. Would it help the cause of justice to have innocent blood spilled? She couldn't discount violence. So many strange things happened these days.

She walked along the corridor and went back down the stairs. It wasn't time to go off duty yet. When she reached the ground floor John appeared before her, and he put out a hand and touched her shoulder briefly, staring into her face with his experienced eyes.

'You're looking shocked,' he said. 'It wasn't a very pleasant experience, was it?'

'It was so sudden,' she said, realising that he thought she was upset by their patient's breakdown. 'We were told to expect something like that, but it was unnerving.'

'It's the first reaction that he's shown to our treatment,' he mused, sounding pleased. 'Your father will be happy about it. But what about you? Will you feel like going out this evening after what happened?'

'Yes, please!' Aileen eyes showed her feelings, and he smiled and took hold of her hand, squeezing it gently.

'Good!' His voice was little more than a whisper, and the smile that came to his face told Aileen more than she could ever have hoped for. 'I shall be finished here myself in a short while, so we'll be able to get away soon. I've rung for two tickets at the

Summer Show on at the Pavilion Theatre. The second house starts at eight-fifteen. This is going to be our first real night out, Aileen.'

'I'm looking forward to it,' she retorted.

'See you at seven. I've got one or two things to do before I can call it a day, so I'd better run along.'

She watched him going, and there were lights in her eyes. When Sister Preston's voice sounded at her back she was startled, and turned quickly, but she found a half-smile upon her superior's face that belied the harsh tone.

'Nurse, are you going to stand there until you are relieved?' Sister Preston demanded.

'No, Sister!'

'We're short-handed now Nurse Gould has gone off duty. See what you can do to help Nurse Collins. You'll have plenty of time when you get finished to think of your evening out.'

Aileen smiled and went off quickly. But as she allowed her mind to return to thoughts of Angela she could not hold on to the warm feelings of happiness that had gripped her while she spoke to John. Her brow furrowed as she sought Sally Collins. What could be done about Angela?

From then until she was relieved was a drag, and Aileen kept glancing at her watch and wondering if it had stopped. She was eager to go out with John, but afraid of the evening's events that lay ahead. Was there any need to fear Allan Belfield? Why was the man so afraid of getting caught? Why had he permitted Angela to accompany him if he was so worried that his misdemeanours would be discovered? She frowned as she tried to formulate some theory that would give credence to his actions. But there seemed no likely explanation.

Her relief at getting off duty did much to restore her high spirits, and she hurried up to her room to take a shower and prepare for the evening out. She looked into Joanne Gould's room as she returned to her own, and was surprised to see the girl lying awake.

'You're supposed to be asleep,' she said severely. 'But how are you feeling now?'

'Much better. It was quite a shock.' Joanne sighed as she stared at Aileen. 'You're seeing Doctor Lindsay this evening, aren't you?' There was a slightly warmer note in the girl's tones, and Aileen noticed it. Perhaps the shock the girl had received with Paul Raynor had startled her out of her habitual manner.

'I am,' she replied.

"You're lucky. I had hopes in that direction once myself. But you're a nice girl, Aileen. I'm sorry for the way I acted towards you. I'm not a very nice girl to know. I've had a hard life and I don't like to think about it. I'm hard inside and I act that way towards everyone.'

'We can't help what befalls us on the road through life,' Aileen said a little awkwardly. She could tell that Joanne was still partly under the influence of the sedative that had been given her. 'I'm sure we're all a little churlish at times.'

'It wasn't my fault,' Joanne said slowly, closing her eyes. 'But you're not making the same mistake I did. I tried for Doctor Lindsay and failed, and I went to Allan Belfield as second best. He certainly is second best. But you've got a better chance, Aileen, and you should make the most of it. I saw you with Belfield the night before last. Don't be so silly as to go with him again. He hasn't caught you, has he? That's how he hooked me, by taking me out one evening. He's fond of nurses, and it took me a considerable time to find out why. Now I know it's too late for me, but it isn't for you. Stay away from him, Aileen, or he'll make you rue the day you were born.'

Joanne's eyes closed, her voice trailing off as she fell under the influence of the sedative again. Aileen realised that the girl hadn't really known what she had been saying, and she bent over her, touching a shoulder gently in an effort to arouse her. But Joanne was asleep, breathing deeply, and Aileen stared at the girl with speculation in her wide blue eyes. What had Joanne meant by her words? Was there some kind of mystery about Allan Belfield that needed solving?

CHAPTER ELEVEN

By the time Aileen was ready to go down and meet John her mind was in a turmoil. She was certain that Joanne had said more than she intended, and what the girl had told her added up to a basis for suspecting the man and his motives. If Belfield had turned Joanne into what she was, then his companionship was undesirable. But what had the girl meant when she spoke of finding out Belfield's reason for wanting to get to know nurses? That sounded ominous, and proved that his meeting with Angela the night before last could not have been an accident. But how would he know a nurse when he saw one out of uniform? Aileen had a sudden picture of Pat Carmell's face in her mind, and she exhaled deeply as the answer came to her. Of course, Carmell would point out the nurses to Belfield. But what made nurses so desirable to the man?

On her way down to the doctors' room to call for John, Aileen met Sister Preston, but her mind was so engrossed with her thoughts that she didn't see her superior. It wasn't until the Sister spoke that Aileen realised she was there, and she stopped short and mentally shook herself from her mind's power.

'I'm sorry, Sister, I was thinking,' she apologised.

'Well! If you're like this on duty, then I'll have to make arrangements to have you replaced,' Sister Preston said, but there was a twinkle in her dark eyes. 'So that's what love can do, is it? Well, all I can say is that I'm glad it's you and not your sister who fell for Doctor Lindsay. I was on my way up to see you. Because Nurse Gould is unfit for duty I'm changing the duty lists around. I'm bringing one of the relief nurses in tomorrow and giving you your day off. Will that be all right? You haven't made arrangements to go out on Friday, have you?'

'No, Sister. It will be all right.'

'Good. I like to please my staff, but these alterations cannot be helped. Is your sister in her room?'

'No, she went out.'

'Well, tell her when you see her that she will have tomorrow night off duty, and she'll come back on to day shift on Friday. But I hope she's going to behave herself now.'

'I've tried to talk some sense into her,' Aileen admitted.

'I know. I can see that it's of little use. She should have more thought for her father.'

'She may learn in time.'

The Sister nodded and turned away. 'Have a nice evening,' she called over her shoulder, and Aileen smiled.

John was waiting for her in the doctors' room, and he took her arm as they walked along the corridors. Aileen felt some of her tension draining away, but there was a thick layer of worry in her mind that no amount of hope and love could shift. When they reached John's car he paused and glanced at her.

'Are you sure you're feeling all right?' he

demanded. 'Would you like to call off this evening's trip?'

'No' she said quickly. She felt that if she didn't get away for a spell she would go mad. 'I'm perfectly all right. But am I looking peaky?'

'Yes.' He smiled. 'But a diversion should snap you out of it. I'm very pleased, myself, that the incident occurred this afternoon, because it means that Paul Raynor's mind is going over to the offensive. That's the sign we've been waiting for. He should start making progress in the right direction now.'

'All's well that ends well!' Aileen quoted. 'But Joanne Gould took quite a shock.'

'All in a day's work,' he said.

They got into the car and he drove out of the grounds. Aileen found herself sighing deeply in relief as they reached the open road and he sent the car fast towards the town. A burden seemed to be lifting from her shoulders, and she straightened herself and began to take an interest in her surroundings.

'Feeling better?' John asked suddenly. 'I heard that sigh of yours. I wish you'd tell me what's on your mind, Aileen. I can tell that you're worried about something.'

'It's nothing that I should want to worry you with,' she replied. 'I think it will sort itself out.'

'Angela again.' He nodded. 'I haven't had the chance to talk to her yet, but she's got a lecture due from me and I'll see that she gets it.'

'Sister Preston told me Angela is coming back on days,' Aileen commented. 'You'll get your chance then.'

They went into Whitebay, and Aileen could not help wondering where her sister was. Then a thought struck her and she turned cold. Would Angela get back to Fairlawns in time to go on duty? She suffered new worry as the thought opened up fresh avenues of conjecture. But she thrust them aside as John parked the car. She took his arm as they walked towards the theatre amidst the people thronging the sea front, and John kept glancing down at her, smiling warmly. She could see the pleasure in his eyes, and knew that he was falling in love with her. The knowledge made her happy, and but for the nagging worries in her mind she would have been the happiest girl in the world.

John brought her a box of chocolates, and when it was time they entered the theatre and sat watching the show. Aileen began to lose herself in the entertainment, and her worries relaxed their hold upon her mind.

She laughed at the patter of the comedians, and didn't notice that John was watching her very closely, enjoying himself now she was at last showing pleasure.

During the interval John asked her if she wanted a drink in the nearby licensed bar, and Aileen was about to agree when a voice spoke over the microphone on the stage. She was amazed to hear John's name called.

'If Doctor Lindsay of Fairlawns Convalescent Home is in the audience will he please go to the manager's office?'

The announcement was repeated as they stared at each other, and then dismay came to John's face.

'How do they know you're here?' Aileen asked as they prepared to leave.

'I told Sister Preston we were coming here this evening. They always like to know where I am, just in case of emergency. I expect it's to do with Paul Raynor. Perhaps I should have stayed behind this evening, but I was so keen to get out with you.'

'My father is on duty,' Aileen said.

'But I'm handling Raynor's case personally. I'm sorry about this, Aileen.'

'There's no need to be sorry,' she replied with a smile. 'I spoiled our first two dates, didn't I?'

'Well, it seems to be a fact that we can't get an uninterrupted evening together,' he replied, taking her arm. 'But this may not be serious. Perhaps they want some information or something.'

Aileen remained silent, and waited in the foyer when John went to the manager's office. Tense moments passed before he returned, and one look at his grim face told her that something was seriously wrong.

'I shall have to go back to Fairlawns,' he said. 'Raynor has had some form of brainstorm. He went beserk a few minutes ago and they had trouble restraining him. They've got him under sedation now, but your father feels that I should be there.'

'Certainly!' Aileen said quickly. 'Come along.'

'I'm sorry about this evening,' he said slowly, 'but the manager says we can have complimentaries to come and see the rest of the show another evening.'

Aileen smiled and squeezed his hand to show that she didn't mind, and they left the theatre and hurried to his car. On the drive back to Fairlawns they were both silent, and Aileen glanced at her watch. The time was nine-thirty. Angela should be on duty now.

'It's a good thing we had that trouble from

Raynor this afternoon,' John said suddenly, showing that his mind was fully occupied by what was happening at Fairlawns. 'If he hadn't been in that security room this evening there might have been the dickens of a row.'

'Didn't you expect another mental seizure?' Aileen asked.

'There's no telling what might happen when a patient is under such complicated treatment,' he replied, and lapsed into silence. Aileen remained silent out of respect for his thoughts.

When they reached Fairlawns John parked his car at the front of the building and helped Aileen out of the seat before leading the way into the building with long strides.

'See you later, Aileen,' he said, making for the Sister's office for the latest report. 'I'm sorry about this evening, but we'll make up for it later, won't we?'

'Many times,' she replied warmly, and for a moment their glances met and an untold message flashed between them. Aileen felt her heart warm to him. There was so much promise in his gaze. 'I'll have an early night,' she said as they parted. 'It has been a tiring day.'

'See you in the morning then.' He paused

and came back to her, taking her swiftly into his arms and kissing her. 'Aileen, I'm falling in love with you,' he said softly. 'I've had you in my thoughts all today, and nothing seems to be able to shift you. That's a healthy sign, isn't it?'

'Only if the girl responds, otherwise it's a dreadful thing,' she replied without thinking, and then she saw the pain in his eyes and remembered what her father had told her. 'I'm sorry,' she said quickly. 'Perhaps I shouldn't have said that.'

'Why not?' He stared at her. 'It's the plain truth, isn't it? A man should find out how the girl feels before he begins to make plans. How do you feel about me, Aileen?'

His arms around her were like steel bands, and she looked up into his face with wide blue eyes. She smiled, and he seemed to relax a little, taking it for a favourable sign.

'I think I'm falling in love with you, John,' she whispered.

He kissed her again, this time more passionately, and she gave herself up to him. They clung together until an apologetic cough sounded in the background. They moved apart quickly, both turning in surprise, and Aileen saw her father standing there, a smile on his face.

'Sorry to interrupt,' he said benignly. 'But I really do need you, John.'

'Coming at once,' John replied, and glanced at Aileen as he hurried forward. His brown eyes told her much, and Aileen nodded slowly, answering his unspoken question. She watched them out of sight, then sighed shudderingly and turned to go up to her room. At that moment she was deliriously happy.

There was a figure moving in the top corridor, and it startled Aileen as she turned a corner and spotted it suddenly. Then she recognised Joanne Gould, and paused at her door as the nurse came towards her.

'Can't you sleep, Joanne?' she demanded.

'I've got a guilty conscience,' Nurse Gould replied. 'I can't sleep properly at any time.'

Aileen narrowed her eyes as she studied the distraught face before her. The girl was still suffering the shock effects of the incident that had occurred that afternoon.

'You'd better get back to bed,' she said kindly. 'Can I get you something?'

'No thank you. Why are you back so early? You were going to the show this evening, weren't you?'

'We went, and were called out during the interval. Paul Raynor has had another violent fit.'

Joanne Gould gasped and lifted a hand to her throat. Aileen stared at the girl.

'I'm sorry, I shouldn't have mentioned his name,' she said. 'You had a bad scare this afternoon.'

'It isn't that,' Joanne replied slowly. 'It's something I've done. I'm sure it's affected Paul Raynor's recovery.'

'What on earth are you talking about?' Aileen watched the girl's face, and for a moment she wondered if the incident that afternoon had affected Joanne's reason. The girl's dark eyes were wild-looking, her face showing great distress. Aileen stepped forward and put an arm about the girl's shoulder. 'Come along,' she said seriously. 'Into bed with you. I'll get you some aspirin. What you need is a good night's sleep.'

'Do you know that Angela didn't come back for her duty this evening?' Joanne demanded.

'What?' Aileen stared at the girl. 'You're joking!'

'I'm not! I only wish I were!'

Aileen stood still, staring at the girl, and something in her face must have meant something to Joanne Gould. The girl uttered a cry and turned wearily away. Aileen went after her, and Joanne was so unsteady that she had to be supported by Aileen's arms. They entered the girl's room and Aileen managed to get her to the bed. Joanne flopped down upon it and lay back, her eyes closed. She was breathing shallowly, and Aileen began to feel alarmed. She felt for the girl's pulse, but her action aroused Joanne. The girl sat up, wrenching her arm away.

'I'm not ill,' she said thinly. 'I'm sick with worry, yes, but that's not illness. I'm in the most awful trouble I've ever known, and your sister is going along the same path.'

'What do you mean, Joanne?' Aileen demanded, sitting down on the foot of the bed and studying the girl's tense face. 'You said something earlier, when you were almost delirious, that made me think. You said you know Allan Belfield. What does that man mean to you? Why are you so upset? Why does Belfield want to get to know nurses?'

Joanne stared at her for a moment, then burst into tears. Aileen shook her head, sighing impatiently. The news that Angela hadn't showed up for night duty was heavy inside her, and she wondered why her father hadn't mentioned it when they met. But he was concerned about their patient. Staff troubles were secondary, even though they might be personal.

'Where does Belfield live?' she demanded suddenly.

'Why?' Joanne looked at her with tear-filled eyes.

'Because Angela must be with him and someone has to go and fetch her. She was out driving with him the other night, and said she couldn't remember half what happened.'

'She said that?' Joanne sat stiffly, staring at Aileen with fear showing in her face. Then she let her shoulders sag, and she slumped back on the bed, defeat coming into her eyes. 'So it's happened to her, too.'

'What's happened to her, Joanne?' Aileen resisted the impulse to seize hold of the girl by the shoulders and shake some life into her.

'It's all my fault, I suppose,' Joanne went on, and there was a note of unreality in her tones. 'Belfield could see that I was reaching the stage where I didn't care any more. So that's why he didn't bother. He decided to get himself a fresh girl.'

'A fresh girl for what? Are you in love with Belfield, Joanne?'

'Never! I've always hated him. I was greatly tempted more than once to give him some poison instead of what he asked for.' She laughed bitterly. 'Perhaps that would have been the easiest way out in the long run.'

'Don't talk in riddles, Joanne. Please tell me what's wrong. Is Angela in any danger?'

'Of course she is. Belfield duped me into doing what he wanted, and now I won't help him any more he's got your sister to carry on the dirty work.'

'What do you mean?' There was alarm growing inside Aileen, and she shook Joanne by the shoulders. Footsteps were sounding in the corridor, and she glanced towards the open door, but saw no one. 'Joanne, you must tell me what's on your mind.'

'I shall have to tell someone,' the girl said slowly. 'It has become a nightmare to me. I've changed completely in these past few months. I've been stealing drugs and giving them to Allan Belfield.'

'What!' Aileen almost choked over the word, and she stared in speechless wonder at the girl. Joanne was stiff-faced, wooden, and now she had cleared the most import-ant hurdle she began to talk freely. There was bitterness in her tones, and a glitter of hatred in her eyes.

'Belfield tricked me. I met him through

Pat Carmell, the day porter. There was an evening when I didn't know the half of what happened, just like your sister told you. But later I was told some of the things I was supposed to have done. It took me a long time to figure out that Belfield had lied just to get me into his power. By then it was too late. I was already stealing drugs for him. There was ample opportunity here. I used to dilute some of the drugs to replace the stolen quantities, and Paul Raynor didn't get half the amounts he was prescribed. I think that's why he acted as he did this afternoon. I've been trying to pluck up courage for a long time to tell someone, to get it off my conscience, but it's a difficult thing to do. I have to confess that I've broken every rule and oath a nurse knows.'

Aileen was aware of a rising hope in her heart. Perhaps Angela hadn't been guilty of knocking down that cyclist! But the thought was at the back of her mind. Her attention was occupied by what Joanne had said.

'You must make a complete confession immediately,' she said. 'Paul Raynor is suffering another of those fits. I must tell Doctor Lindsay immediately. Joanne, there's a chance for you to put matters right. You've done wrong and no one can condone it, but you can lessen the evil a little by telling what you know. Will you do that?'

'Yes!' The girl's tone was strong. 'It's all that's left to me.'

'And Angela!' Aileen's heart seemed to miss a beat. 'Where would I find her, do you think?'

'Belfield has a beach chalet near the pier. It's called *Seaview*. It's the third one along from the pier, standing in its own grounds and with a high wooden fence around three sides of it. A car can drive right up to the back of it. That's where Belfield will likely be at this time, and no doubt your sister is with him.'

There was a sharp tapping at the door and Aileen spun around, gasping in surprise when she saw the tall, uniformed figure of the local constable standing in the doorway.

'Excuse me,' he said grimly. 'I came up here to get a few more details of what happened last night, but I couldn't help overhearing what was said. If you wish to make a statement, Nurse Gould, then you'd better get dressed and come with me.'

Aileen got to her feet. Joanne sprang up from the bed and began to remove her dressing gown.

'I'll be with you in a few moments,

Constable,' she said. 'Just give me time to get dressed.'

'Tell everything, Joanne,' Aileen said firmly. 'It's the only way. I'd better tell Doctor Lindsay about Paul Raynor's drugs dosages.'

The constable stepped out of the doorway, nodding at her as she passed him.

'Lucky I was on hand,' he remarked. 'I heard it all. I stood listening at the door when I heard voices. I think the police at Whitebay will be pleased to have something to pin on Allan Belfield. They've been troubled by his activities for quite some time.'

Aileen nodded and hurried away, almost running down the stairs. Now all she could think of was her sister. She was breathless when she reached the ground floor, and her heart was pounding fiercely. She saw John coming along the corridor, and he turned into the Sister's office without seeing her. Aileen hurried after him, filled with a sense of growing urgency. He was alone in the office when she burst in upon him, and she saw surprise come to his face as he looked up. She quickly blurted out what she had learned from Joanne Gould, and pure astonishment filtered into his expression as he listened. He got to his feet and came around the desk, his face grim, his dark eyes filled with worry.

'That could account for the mysteries in Raynor's case,' he said. 'I must talk to your father about this, Aileen. But you've been worried about Angela, haven't you? You thought she had knocked down that cyclist in that stolen car?'

'It might still be true,' she said slowly. 'But whatever happened, it will come out now. May I borrow your car, John? I'd like to go into town and try and find Angela before she gets too deeply involved with this man.'

'You have a current licence?' he demanded, and she nodded. 'Then take it by all means, but be careful, won't you? I wish I could go with you but I'm tied here.'

'Thank you, but I'll manage on my own.' Aileen held out her hand for the keys, and he drew her into his arms before handing them over.

'Aileen, I think you're the most wonderful girl in the world,' he said slowly. 'You must have had a dreadful burden on your mind. Your face showed it at times. But it's over now, if you're right in what you say. The police will soon straighten out matters. Then we'll be able to look forward to a normal relationship, shan't we?'

'No interruptions,' she said, smiling.

'Nothing to worry about. That sounds like Heaven!'

'It sounds like the place we'll move into,' he retorted, and then he sighed. 'But I must get back to your father.'

'Don't tell him about Angela,' she begged. 'I may be able to extricate her from the worst of this. But that remains to be seen.'

'I shan't say anything,' he replied, smiling gently. 'You go and do your best, sweetheart.'

Aileen took his car keys and hurried out to the front of the house. Her heart was pounding as she slid into the vehicle. It was a strange model and she had to check for light switches and ignition. In the darkness her hands fumbled, and she shook her head impatiently. Then she took a firm grip upon her leaping impulses and started the car. A few moments later she was driving slowly towards the road, and when she reached it she sent the car on at great speed. As she drove her mind churned over all that Joanne had told her, and she smiled grimly as she pictured the distraught girl making a complete confession to the police. It seemed that Allan Belfield's threats would not avail him at all now.

But she was worried by her sister's failure to return to Fairlawns. What did it mean?

Had Angela decided against helping Belfield despite the pressure he was applying? What would he do to get his own way? She shuddered to think, recalling the way he had spoken to her. He was not a nice character to know, and she hoped that if Angela came out of this all right her sister would have learned her lesson.

When she reached Whitebay she drove along the sea front, and slowed at a pedestrian crossing to permit some holiday-makers to cross. A figure ran into the road beside the car and waved at her, and Aileen looked hard and recognised Sally Collins. The nurse came to the side window.

'Aileen,' she gasped in surprise. 'I recognised the car and hoped to get a lift back to Fairlawns. But where's John?'

'That's a long story, Sally,' Aileen retorted. 'But jump in. I shall be going back to Fairlawns shortly. I'm looking for Angela. She came to town earlier and didn't get back to go on duty.'

Sally hurriedly got into the car at her side, and Aileen drove on, telling the girl about Joanne's disclosures, and the nurse kept gasping in shock as each detail was made known. Aileen even told her about Angela and the fears they had of the accident which had occurred.

'Good Lord, Aileen, it's a wonder you didn't go out of your head with worry! What a fool that sister of yours is! But you shouldn't be doing this, you know. It could be dangerous. I've heard all about Allan Belfield. He definitely isn't the kind of man any girl would willingly get entangled with.'

'My foolish sister always asks for trouble, and she's certainly got it this time. All I hope is that she isn't too deeply incriminated.' Aileen swung the car off the small road leading down from the sea front to the access road behind the row of beach chalets, and brought it to a halt at the rear of the third holiday villa. She saw lights at some of the windows, and spotted Angela's car drawn up in the shadows nearby. Relief swept through her, and she started out of the car. 'You'd better wait here for me, Sally,' she said. 'This man is most unpleasant.'

'All the more reason why you should have someone to back you up,' the girl retorted. 'Remember this afternoon? I handled Paul Raynor all right, didn't I?'

Aileen sighed, but made no more comment. They went through the darkness to the door of the chalet, and there was a pounding of excitement in Aileen's breast as she knocked at the door. Several moments passed. She could hear the sound of pop music coming from inside the little building, and she glanced at Sally, who shrugged.

'Seems as if Angela finds this more attractive than doing her stint of night duty,' Sally said grimly. 'Hello, here comes an answer.'

A light flooded the immediate area outside the door, and Aileen saw a man's figure through the thick glass panels of the door. The next instant the door was opened and Pat Carmell stared out at them.

'What the devil are you doing here?' he demanded blearily, blinking from one to the other.

'I've come for Angela,' Aileen said. 'You know she should be on night duty.'

'She's old enough to make up her own mind to what she wants to do,' Carmell retorted. 'But come on in and join the party. You two aren't on duty.'

Aileen followed him as he stepped back into the building and Sally went along behind, slamming the door at her back. They entered a large lounge, and Aileen blinked at the bright lights. She saw Angela seated on a sofa beside Allan Belfield, and there was a strange girl across the room attending to the record player.

'Turn that thing off!' Belfield yelled at the girl then he saw Aileen, and sudden silence flooded the room.

Angela stared at Aileen without comment. Pat Carmell went across the room to where his girl was standing, and Sally ranged herself beside Aileen.

'I'm glad you've come,' Belfield said. 'It'll save me a trip to Fairlawns tonight to talk to you. Normally I wouldn't bother talking to you again after that first warning I gave you. But I've taken a real liking to your twin sister, and out of love for her I'll give you another chance so long as you forget this idea of talking to the police.'

'It's not me you've got to worry about talking to the police,' Aileen said thinly.

'What do you mean?' The good-natured act fell from him like a cloak. He got to his feet and came forward to confront Aileen, and she stared boldly at him. 'If you've ignored the warning I gave you then you'll pay for it,' he said ominously.

'Joanne Gould!' Aileen said no more, and she saw his face change expression.

'What about her?' His tones were guarded.

'She's talking to the police right now about what you've made her do.' Aileen laughed at him. 'So you can forget your little plot to involve my sister with your crooked, beastly plans.'

There was a heavy silence as Aileen finished, and Angela was staring at her with surprise marring her lovely, petulant face. Belfield was shocked into ice, and it was Carmell who broke the tension. He started forward from the far side of the room, his face showing fear.

'I'm getting out of here,' he said quickly. 'You're a fool, Allan. I told you this business would make trouble for you.'

'Don't be a fool,' Belfield snarled. 'She's bluffing. I think she's just trying to get her sister off the hook. All right, you can have her. I don't think she's my type. Get her out of here and keep her away from me.'

'Come on, Angela,' Aileen said instantly. 'You've got a lot of talking to do when you get back to Fairlawns. Father will want to know why you didn't go on duty at nine.'

'She's finished with nursing,' Belfield said. 'I talked her into taking a job as a hostess in a club I've got an interest in. That will pay her more than she's getting at Fairlawns.'

'You won't be around to find out,' Aileen said. 'I've told you that the police are learning everything from Joanne Gould.'

'You're bluffing,' he jeered.

'She can't be,' Pat Carmell said in rising tones of panic. 'How does she know about Joanne?'

Belfield's face was changing expression as his mind went to work. Aileen called to Angela, wanting to get away before Belfield turned nasty. But Angela seemed not impressed by what had been said. At that moment there was another loud knocking at the door.

'The police,' Carmell yelped. 'I'm getting out of here.'

'Don't be a fool!' Belfield snapped. His eyes were showing an ugly expression. 'We can bluff this out.'

'Try it,' Aileen told him. 'Let them in and try and talk your way out of this. And while you're at it tell me the truth about what happened the other night? Who was driving the car when that cyclist was knocked down?'

'What cyclist?' he demanded as Carmell walked around him to answer the door. 'If that's the police then you'd better not start talking about things like that. I don't want to get done for something we didn't do. We didn't steal a car. I borrowed it in order to bluff your sister. I doped her a little, and when she came to I told her about the accident. It was just coincidence that one happened the same night. It's the same bluff I've worked before. So you'd better forget about that.'

'You despicable cad!' Angela was on her feet in an instant. She came forward and slapped Belfield's face, the sound of the blow echoing across the room. He turned on her, his arm upraised, but Sally stepped forward and caught his wrist. The next instant he was yelling out in pain, powerless in the girl's strong grip.

Carmell came back into the room followed closely by two uniformed policemen, and Sally released Belfield and dusted her palms together. Aileen put an arm around Angela's shoulders, and there was a pang of relief inside her as the policeman arrested Belfield. A third policeman appeared in the doorway, and there were sounds of other men outside.

Belfield was led away, his face showing bravado, but his eyes proclaimed his fear. A sergeant entered and stared at the female faces watching him. He smiled at Aileen and Angela.

'I was told to watch out for you two,' he said. 'It seems you've played no small part in putting a stop to this business. You'll have to come along to the station with us, but I'm sure you won't be detained long.'

'I have a car outside, and so does my sister,' Aileen said. 'Can we follow you?'

'By all means! Come along.'

They left the chalet, and in the darkness Aileen saw three police cars. One was already leaving, containing Belfield and the arresting officers. Sally accompanied Aileen, who paused as Angela got into her little red sports car.

'You've got nothing to answer for,' she said thinly, 'except why you failed to report for night duty. You should think yourself extremely fortunate, Angela, and if this hasn't taught you a lesson then you deserve all you get. This is the last time I try and help you.'

'I've learned my lesson this time,' her sister replied miserably. 'I'm sorry, Aileen.'

'You always say that, but this time you'd better mean it,' Aileen told her. She softened then and patted Angela's slim shoulder. As she crossed to John's car, with Sally at her side, she straightened her shoulders and peered upwards into the velvet night sky, glancing at the bright stars, and there was a prayer on her lips, a double prayer – she hoped her sister had learned her lesson and she was thankful for the precious gift of John

Lindsay. Somewhere up there, she wanted to believe, was the intelligence which had found enough wisdom to decide that she and John should meet, and having decided, had brought them together.

The publishers hope that this book has given you enjoyable reading. Large Print Books are especially designed to be as easy to see and hold as possible. If you wish a complete list of our books please ask at your local library or write directly to:

Dales Large Print Books
Magna House, Long Preston,
Skipton, North Yorkshire.
BD23 4ND

This Large Print Book, for people
who cannot read normal print,
is published under the auspices of

THE ULVERSCROFT FOUNDATION

... we hope you have enjoyed this book.
Please think for a moment about those
who have worse eyesight than you ...
and are unable to even read or enjoy
Large Print without great difficulty.

You can help them by sending a
donation, large or small, to:

**The Ulverscroft Foundation,
1, The Green, Bradgate Road,
Anstey, Leicestershire, LE7 7FU,
England.**
or request a copy of our brochure for
more details.

The Foundation will use all donations
to assist those people who are visually
impaired and need special attention
with medical research, diagnosis
and treatment.

Thank you very much for your help.